# LET LOVE HAPPEN

A Novel by

RASHMI JINDAL

INDIA · SINGAPORE · MALAYSIA

ISBN

Hardcase: 979-8-89322-847-2
Paperback: 979-8-89277-828-2

# About the Author

Rashmi Jindal is a passionate and versatile writer. So far, she has published four books, *Fix the Risk of Committing Common Errors in English*, a book on English Grammar; *Athaah- Nari Man aur Jeevan*, and *Harfon ke Paar Chuppiyon pe PhD*, both anthologies of Hindi Poems and her latest fiction book *Let Love Happen*, a romantic novel. Her writing journey began with her first poem at twelve, but it wasn't until eleven years ago that she took it seriously. Besides writing books, she also writes movie scripts.

As Rashmi embarks on her literary journey, she invites readers to delve deep into the pages of her recent novel *Let Love Happen* and experience the enduring magic of love.

For **Papa, Nidhi** and **Adit**

Remember Papa, you used to say my Ruchhu would do something great one day,

maybe this is the beginning.

Hey Nidhi, I owe this to you that I Let Love Happen in my life. Thank you for teaching me to Let Love Happen.

Adit you always used to ask me, "*Bhabhi* when are you publishing your first novel? I want the first copy."

Here it is and your *Bhabhi* feels so helpless …

For the one who is not just one but an epitome of so many things that I cannot pen down; for my friend, love, lifeline, hubby, Manish Jindal.

**Tailor-made**

Whereas I have never been able to fit into the ways of the world,

You always say I am tailor-made for you.

If you are a bud turning into a full-bloom

On a winter morning,

I am dew

Sitting on your petals like a pearl

Sending a chill down you.

You know I cannot be more than this -

A morning dew sitting on a morning bloom,

But you know what I love about you

You close your petals so well,

Engulfing me within you

That though I am not tailor-made

You make me fit into you.

# Contents

# ACKNOWLEDGEMENTS

First, I bow in front of the almighty for everything, especially for providing me with a knack for writing. Writing makes me feel alive, contented, composed, and complete.

I am grateful to all my family members and friends for understanding and allowing me the required space to shape my beloved book. I owe you all a lot. A special thanks to the following:

- A mentor like teacher Dinesh Kumar Sir who appreciated my first short story paving the way for this novel.
- My college friends. In college we were eight friends, everyone endowed with a different talent–Ranjeet, the best singer of the college; Aanchal, the dancing queen; Raminder, the fashion designer; Deepika, the interior decorator; Megha, the best speaker; Manu, a versatile personality and Neha, good at studies and I, the writer–I love you all.
- Principal Sir, MD Ashwani Jindal Sir and my gang at Karan Institute of Technical Education.

Also, my students, though I cannot name all, I remember you all.

- Kurukshetra Institute of Technology and Management that played a great role in shaping my life by giving me the blessings of Director PJ George Sir and MD Sudarshan Agarwal Sir as well as providing me with friends like Meenakshi, Anju Ma'am, Veenu, Sangeeta, sorry I cannot name all but those who mean something to me they know it. Also, the members of my English Club at KITM, I remember you all kiddos; I know you are all grown up now; some are even married, but to me, you will always remain kids.
- My house help, Kanchan, without whom I would never have been able to reach the stage where I am - writing the acknowledgements of this book.
- My darling son. I know I stole time from you for this book. But how you understood and fed me on fresh fruit chats made with your tiny little hands while I was buried neck-deep in the editing work, makes my heart warm. I am so very proud of you, my baby. I promise to compensate for everything.
- My friend, benefactor, guide, and soulmate, Manish Jindal, for keeping me fuelled with hope and enthusiasm whenever I felt overwhelmed; for forcefully listening to the story and my grievances all in the same breath; for putting up with all my eccentricities during the writing and editing process; for always being there for me.

- My readers for loving my stories. My stories and I are nothing without you. I just put my heart and soul into words. You make them complete by giving my stories and verses a place in your hearts. This is the biggest achievement of my life. I can't thank you all enough for this.
- My publisher for making my dream come true.

There is a lot to say about many people I owe something to but as it is not possible to mention every name, I would like to end with love to all the kids in my family. Kids, I feel, are the best creation of God.

# 1

# Giggles, Guffaws and All Things Edible

As I step onto the bus, my rage knows no bounds. One glance at goofy Naina, and I already know who has plotted this. I clench my fists, resisting the urge to strangle her. As I make eye contact with her, my anger evident, I sit down in the only seat left vacant for staff on bus No. 4 of SITE College. My seatmate, flirty-faced Bharat Mittal, the accelerator-*toofani*[1], grins at me. I inhale deeply and force a smile.

Ugh! Every pore of this man reeks of obscenity. He has only to look at you to make you feel naked. I know what Naina will say, "What has he done to be labelled obscene? The poor guy is in love with you." Love my foot! I just can't stand him.

Though Mr Mittal takes all my classes when I need to take leave, I have coined numerous negative adjectives for him, like - flirty-faced, accelerator-*toofani*[1], a man with many hearts and the ever-green Gangudin, to name a few. The first word that fell from my mouth upon meeting him was Gangudin. The entire staff, now my *Chandal Chaukdi*[2], had doubled up with laughter on hearing the word.

As the days passed, he kept ogling me, and I kept inventing new names for him. That was my only form of revenge. However petty, it gave me solace. I named him flirty-faced because he always drools over me with those toad-like eyes. Naina says I am pathetic where boys are concerned, flinching even at harmless advances. And in punishment for my breaking hearts, prophesies Naina, I will get a husband who'll torture me with his love. And so, while I chase my books, he'll chase me.

No matter how much Naina teases me, she is a darling. She is the one who is teaching me to be more expressive. To be more alive. I met her on my very first day at SITE. She thought my *jiju*[3], who had come to drop me off, was my father. She tried to assure him that I would be fine. My sweet *jiju*[3] had merely smiled and not corrected her. In that one meeting, Naina and I became best friends. Right from riding in local buses when no bus service was provided by the college to handling the unruly hooligans, she taught me to smile in every situation. And Saksham Institute of Technical Education became a home away from home for me.

With Naina, everything is fun. But when I learned her story with its three harsh realities, I was flabbergasted. First, Naina's mother is her stepmother and so is her brother. Just yesterday he threw a glass at her, which she ducked from just in time. Second, she had met with a terrible accident when she was just fourteen. Her jaw was displaced and her vocal cords were damaged. Even now she sounds shrill, like Uncle Scrooge from Duck Tales when she speaks. Some people find it funny, but I don't. Naina's heart is pure, and that is all that counts.

I mentioned a third reality. And it is this. She has a best friend named Sid with whom she is madly in love and who loves someone else. Wait! This is not it. Our goofy, helping Naina is his love adviser. She has helped him in getting the girl of his dreams. Sid met with an accident. And Naina advised him to use that accident as blackmail to persuade his parents to accept the girl. Poor parents! For the sake of their child, they arranged their marriage in the hospital itself and showered their blessings on the girl. Naina is nuts. Really! It is rare to find a pure love like hers. Who else would help the love of her life find the love of his life?

Oh God! This whole love thing sucks. I just want to stay away from all this bullshit. I have my books. They are all I need; they demand no sacrifices and cause no pain. But today I'm going to give Naina a good piece of my mind. She is the only person who can arrange for a seat beside Mittal to be empty for me.

My plan of killing Naina will not work today. Naina, food connoisseur Shravan Sir, technical expert Dhingra Sir and Tanmay *bhiaya*[4] have already planned to get down at Ambedkar *Chowk*[5] to eat some *panipuris*[6] from the best *panipuriwala*[7] in the city of Kurukshetra, the land of Mahabharata. I am not keen on joining them but soon follow, glaring at Naina, who continues to revel in my frustration. As soon as we settle on the bench behind the *panipuriwala's*[7] stall, Naina cocks her eyebrows and I stick out my tongue at her.

"These *panipuris*[6] are the best I've ever eaten and they are available in six flavours," food connoisseur, Shravan Sir, begins.

"Who can doubt your expertise on food?" Tanmay *bhaiya*[4], another food enthusiast, adds.

As the discussion on the best foods available in Kurukshetra gets more heated, I sit with my arms crossed over my chest, shoulders slumped, and lips pouted.

"Look at her." Naina attracts everyone's attention to me. "Still sulking," she says.

Four pairs of eyes turn towards me.

"I think we should have invited Mittal also," Naina quips.

"No," I shriek. Naina's mission is successful.

The group bursts into uncontrollable bouts of laughter and soon I join in. Naina hugs me.

"After all, can cream and milk stay separate?" Dhingra Sir declares in his usual all-knowing tone. Soon an array of *panipuris*[6] begins to arrive in mint flavour followed by asafoetida, guava and pomegranate flavours. There is a wonderful camaraderie in the group as we start fighting over the water-filled balls. After we have finished eating, we begin another favourite pastime of ours, cursing Teddy Bear, our honourable Principal Dr Chaube. Finally, it is time to make our way home.

For four months now, life has been quite beautiful at SITE College. Though it is not a big college, not even a prestigious one I dreamed of working in, I look forward to going to this polytechnic institute daily. Not only my *Chandal Chaukdi*[2] but also my students of Computer Engineering dote over me.

Little do I know that this happiness will be short-lived. Soon life is going to take a U-turn. How unpredictable life is. It offers you things you have desired all your life, but sometimes at the cost of those you never want to let go of.

# 2

# THE BORING BUMPY RIDE

After taking lectures for half the day, Naina, Tanmay *bhaiya*[4], Shravan Sir, Dhingra Sir and I are famished.

We put a lot of effort into designing the timetable so that our *Chandal Chaukdi*[2] can enjoy our food together during the fourth lecture. After all, food binds us together.

As we open our *dabbas*[8] ready to snatch the most tempting offering, my phone pings. Sulochana, a friend who works in a nearby engineering college, has been forcing me to join her for an interview at IITM College. It is one of the most reputed engineering colleges in Kurukshetra. After her incessant cajoling, I had given in, though I had forgotten all about it afterwards. As soon as I read her message, 'Ready? Have left?' I choke on the bite of cheese-chilly and *roti*[9] I had just stuffed in my mouth. Naina had been at it again. She had placed green chilly in place of cheese. Now the hiccups are killing me. As I cough, my whole group gaze at me. None of them offers me water because they know how particular I am about drinking my water. While all my gang are quite cool about sharing ice-creams, food, and water, I have a phobia. No *jhootha*[10]! I grab my water bottle, gulp it in one go, grab my handbag and run for the door announcing,

"Taking a half day off."

"Have you applied for leave?" Dhingra Sir calls out.

"Naina will take care of it," I shout, fleeing the room.

At Sulochana's college gate, she's awaiting me. To my surprise, she doesn't appear annoyed.

"So, how's the preparation? Do you think they'll ask questions about Literature?" Sulochana asks.

"Um... mm," I fumble, realising I haven't even considered it.

"You know what Sulu, I'm quite happy in my present job. I don't want to switch," I mumble.

"So, you will rot in a polytechnic college for the rest of your life? What about your dreams?"

"I... I." I keep biting my nails.

We both board a local bus and keep quiet for the rest of the journey. How much fun this ride could be if Naina were there. After half an hour of a boring, bumpy ride, we reach our destination – IITM, Indraprastha Institute of Technology and Management. Sulochana wasn't wrong in singing songs in praise of the college.

The building is quite impressive – bigger and grander than SITE. Passing the beautiful ground adorned with flowers in full bloom, we reach the reception area. It is like the reception of some big hotel with a map of the college displayed on the big front wall. The receptionist, an amiable lady in her mid-thirties, greets us. We take seats in the cool steel waiting chairs. The candidates soon start swarming in. As we chat with them, we realise that most of them have PhDs. Soon, a discussion on the rate of unemployment in our country begins.

PhD holders have now begun applying for jobs as Assistant Professors in engineering colleges. Besides the doctorate holders, there are others with experience teaching at an engineering college like Sulochana. I know I stand no chance, with just four months of experience at a polytechnic college.

Soon the bell begins to summon the candidates. When it's my turn, I am not at all nervous. If the theory is to be believed, you stay relaxed in two situations. One - when you are fully prepared; two - when you are not prepared at all. In my condition, the latter applies..

After greeting the panel members, none of whom I am sure knows anything about English Literature, I take my seat. I answer all the questions confidently. They are mainly related to my bio. When it comes to the negotiation of salary, I quote much more than my present salary. I know I am killing every last hope of being selected, but I don't give a damn.

We leave for our homes. Sulochana is relaxed because she is quite hopeful. I because it's finally over. As we board the local bus, I think of my gang having fun at some popular *chaatwala*[11] or *panipuriwala*[7]. As I am about to grab a seat, my phone buzzes. It's Naina.

"So, what's up?"

"Going home."

"Stop pouting and get down at Hot Millions."

"What? Hot Millions?"

"Yes, you heard it right, Hot Millions, it is," Naina chimes in. "Mittal is throwing a party and insists Rhythima should join us."

"No…" I shriek in the overcrowded bus. Many heads turn towards me. On the line, Naina laughs.

"Monika has got engaged. It's her party," Naina shouts.

I take a deep breath and whisper, "Naina, I'm gonna kill you."

I say goodbye to Sulochana and reach Hot Millions. As I enter, I bump into a shrill body, our Gangudin. My irritation flares up as I find Mittal checking me out.

"Naina." I am about to pounce on Naina when my eyes fall on Monika, our cute little receptionist, all happy and beaming, and I forget my anger.

I give Monika a big hug. Tanmay *bhaiya*$_{4}$, as usual, is playing the big brother, serving snacks and drinks to everyone. Shravan Sir, as usual, is delivering his *gyaan*$_{12}$ on food. I settle in one chair when Mittal speaks.

"Rhythima Ma'am, try the *dosas*$_{13}$ here. They are just scrumptious," Mittal clicks his tongue on the letter 's' as he speaks.

"Um... Err… No thanks, I'm fine." I make a face without looking at him.

"OK, Rhythima *Ji*[73], try the *idlis*[14]," Mittal persists.

"Mittal Sir, why don't you take Rhythima to that table," Naina buts in signalling to a table in the far corner.

"Um… I think I should leave. It's getting late," I excuse myself.

"Naina, you also leave," Tanmay *bhaiya*[4] advises, and we both leave. I refuse to look at Naina.

"Sulking again?" Naina giggles as we settle into the rickety auto-rickshaw.

"Nainaaa Chadhhaaaa. Stop!"

"Sid is going to be a father," Naina announces, struggling to blink away the tears that have collected in her eyes. I feel the best smile in this world is when one smiles through one's tears. And Naina wears that smile as a trophy. My heart melts. I know all her goofing around and teasing is just an attempt to mask her tough realities.

"And you know what? It happened when Sid was in the hospital after that accident, and his girl Surabhi…"

"Wait…. put a break, Naina. You discuss all this with Sid?"

"Look at your face. You've gone red. You'll behave the same way with your husband. Tell me what you are gonna do when he…"

"Naina…" I press my palms against my earlobes. "Stop all this nonsense. I will not marry at all."

"We'll see. But at least you must know about life. You are 25 after all and by God, you don't know a thing." Naina rolls her eyes.

"I'm happy with my books."

"And I know yours will be a great romantic…"

"Nainaaa."

I cover her mouth with my palm and do not let her speak for the rest of the journey.

# 3

# To Resign or Not to Resign That Is the Question

Having my gang around makes the days good. We are planning an Inaugural Day for our four-month-old college. Shravan Sir is the head of the Refreshment Team, Naina of Cultural Activities, Dhingra Sir of Technical Things, Tanmay *bhaiya*[4] is a jack of all trades and I am on the stage. Teddy Bear is all a bundle of nerves. All the chief guests he had planned to invite have turned down his invitation.

The D-Day is here. Teddy Bear has managed to invite a Roadways Minister, Mr Abhay Jindal. He is coming in his helicopter. As I stand near the podium to begin the proceedings, my Computer Engineering students seek permission to touch Mr Jindal's helicopter. When I say no, they reason they won't get a chance to do this in their life again. After a little persuasion, I allow them, not in groups, but one by one. I know my students would never disobey their Rhythima Ma'am. As soon as the Chief Guest arrives, I mount the stage, my territory; the only place besides my books I can handle with ease.

The function goes well. All beam with joy. Teddy Bear has no idea how to control the grin that's plastered all over his face. My *Chandal Chaukdi*[2] helped him a lot in making the function a success, and he can't thank us enough. Just as we are revelling in our success, I get a call from an unknown number that's about to change my life.

I don't know whether I should be happy or sad after receiving the call. Out of all the applicants for the Assistant Professor position at IITM, I have been selected, and they are even offering me the exact amount of money I requested.

Naina knows something is amiss. In the middle of all the merriment, I am sulking. She corners me to get the truth out of me.

In the evening, we all get down at Dhingra Sir's internet café shop to discuss my plight. To my sheer surprise, Naina, of all the people, is forcing me to go ahead, though her eyes are glistening with tears.

With Naina's counsel and support from all, we have made the decision–I'll apply for resignation tomorrow. The catch is, I have to join IITM on the second of February 2009 and today is the 31st of January.

*No! My heart will break!*

♥♥♥

## Next Day

I am sitting in my Language Lab with my resignation ready at my table. Thanks to Tanmay *bhaiya*[4] for doing the typing bit as my hands won't move. All my gang members are hovering over me. Naina is shouting at me while others are trying to put some sense in my head that I should not turn down the offer. They all know it's always been my dream to do PhD and work in some graduate college where I can teach English Literature. Yeah, I'm also preparing for UGC NET to fulfil this dream. But you never know and should always have a backup plan. The job at the engineering college could serve as experience for future endeavours, while my role in a polytechnic college wouldn't.

As we all are busy in our ruckus, Sarika Ma'am saunters in. She has such a big nose that she can sniff from a 10 km distance what's going on. In her typical accent, she interjects,

"So Riiithiiiima madam, rejaining today? (So Rhythima Ma'am, resigning today?)"

We gasp! *How on earth does she know?*

Sarika Ma'am is the one who keeps trying to get into our group, and we keep resisting. In the past, she had tried to bully us all, especially me, as she is my senior, and also a faculty in English. She would make me take even her classes and when the students of her class began to demand to be taught by me, she became my rival. Ignoring her duties, she always keeps on trying to flatter the Management.

All leave to take their respective classes. I am left alone to ponder over the issue at hand, resign or not to resign. That's true that I am quite attached to my present workplace and I enjoy here a lot, but that's also true that I want to move on in life and do something big. Half of the day has passed. Naina, Mittal and even Sarika Ma'am have taken care of all my lectures. I sneak inside MD Sir's office to drop my resignation letter. But as soon as I enter his office, I find the room swarmed with the students of Computer Engineering. They seem to be on some sort of strike. A few have even tears in their eyes.

As I am about to turn to go, MD Sir calls me, asking me to show what's there in my hand. The small A4 size piece of paper seems to be heavy as a paperweight as I extend my hand to hand over the resignation letter. He takes the paper and keeps it aside, announcing,

"You are not going anywhere."

The students return to their classes relaxed. I am sitting in front of MD Sir, tongue-tied.

"So Rhythima Ma'am, you didn't even consider discussing with us, but told the students."

*Oh, God! MD Sir is offended.*

"No sir, I swear I never told them. I didn't take a single class today. I know they are attached to me," I trail off.

"I know… I know. Sarika Ma'am took your class today and told them and they all barged in here requesting us to turn down your resignation."

"I don't know how Sarika Ma'am… I never told her." *How do I explain to sir that all this thing was just unplanned? It just happened?* I am so choked with emotions. I know my students are attached to me, but I never had an idea that the entire class would throng MD Sir's office requesting to keep me.

"OK, let's come to the point. We are quite impressed with your spirit of work, so we are ready to increase your salary."

*Oh God, why is it all sounding so materialistic? Why sir is not talking to me in the same fatherly tone he always does?*

*You are pathetic Rhythima. How long will you continue searching for your father in other people? You need to grow. Even after increasing, the salary they offer you is not half of what IITM is offering you.*

Tears have pooled in my eyes. I can't take it anymore. I just request to be excused. As I make my way to my lab, I find all my students already gathered there. They plead with me not to leave them. Abhay, my favourite, comes forward and speaks on behalf of the entire class,

"Ma'am, you are the one who instilled us with confidence. You gave us self-reliance that even our parents never did. Please don't leave us."

I still can't utter a word. *Why am I so horrible at talking about emotions? Why do I keep choking when I am too filled with emotions?* Suddenly some footsteps are heard and all know it's Sarika Ma'am. She is more than happy with my leaving college. What won't she give to have me thrown out of her way?

"Oye, (Hey, listen,)" she starts in her peculiar accent, "Lat ar goo. Iph see ad loved ju pipl in fast pilace si had not applied in IITM. See phancij big college, lat ar goo. (Let her go. If she had loved you people in the first place, she would not have applied to IITM. She fancies big college, let her go.)"

"Why didn't you apply Sarika Ma'am?" Sachin buts in. I give him a sharp look and he shuts his mouth.

Sarika Ma'am is suddenly flustered, her ears all red, and she stomps out of the lab.

"She had applied, but she didn't even get a call for the interview. She even tried to use her husband's links," Aakash, who lives near Sarika Ma'am's house, informs us. And things start falling into place how she knows. Naina walks in, a whirlwind of emotions bundled within her. If there is an award for an honest display of emotions, Naina will get it. In front of the whole class of 60 students, she pounces on me with teary eyes,

"How can you go Rhythima when all are asking you not to, and they are even increasing your salary? I'd not have given up all this love even in return for crores of rupees."

"B... but Naina, you were the one who..."

"Yes, I was, but only till I didn't know they all love you so much. Only till I didn't know you have got something much richer than money here. At that time, I didn't want to sound selfish by checking you, but now it's not only me." Her lips quiver, showing the silent struggle to hold back the emotion welling up inside. She can't speak any more.

*Oh, Naina darling!*

I give her a tight hug, assuring her that I'll withdraw my resignation by tomorrow morning.

We mount the bus with a heavy heart. We know how the Management, even Teddy Bear, dotes over me and my work, but we also know Sarika Ma'am and her husband's links and how capable she is of foul-playing.

# 4

## LETTING GO OF

It's a new morning. I've decided to take my resignation back. As we all get down from the bus and enter the college, I run into Indu, Sulochana's younger sister. I am very excited to see her, but she seems a little hesitant. I run to take my class as I am dying to announce to my students that I am not going anywhere.

After class, I just fidget to make my way to MD Sir's office to take my resignation back, but he is damn busy today. The usually accessible office seems like the President's Residence today. In all these four months of college, MD Sir has never been this busy. *What's keeping him so busy today?* I have not even had a word with any of my gang members. *What's going on?* After waiting for too long, I still could not have a word with MD Sir. it's lunchtime. At least I will get to see my *Chandal Chaukdi*[2].

As we all sit for lunch in my lab, my *Chandal Chaukdi*[2] seems rather low. No food snatching, no Naina teasing, and no food *gyaan*[12] from Dhingra Sir. All seem to be in deep thought when Naina breaks the ice.

"So done!" She is boiling.

*Done? what's she talking about?*

"Why all that drama yesterday when you had everything planned?" Naina questions sarcastically.

"What plan?"

"Look who's playing...."

"What are you talking about, Naina?" I am perplexed.

Naina just looks away, her eyes glistening.

"OK, I need to run. I have a class."

"What class?" Naina mocks.

"My class."

"You know nothing?"

"What are you talking about, Naina? I am getting late?"

"OK, go," she yells.

I storm out of the lab. Tanmay *bhaiya*[4] attempts to call out but I will not listen. With every step towards room No. 101, my heart sinks. I know I am late, still my feet feel heavy, and they are not ready to move fast. As I reach room No. 101, I am shocked - Indu, Sulochana's sister, is taking my class. Now the truth dawns upon me. It was Sulochana's strategy from day one. I knew she was trying to get her sister appointed in her college, but this I had never thought was in her mind.

I come back to my lab with heavier steps. I plonk in my chair. My head is reeling.

"Happy? How can you be so materialistic, Rhythima?" Naina yells, tears visible in her eyes. More than her, I need a hug right now. I rush to the lady's room and cry my heart out. Naina follows me. She hugs me.

"Who'll take my side now when people will make fun of my Uncle Scrooge's voice," she demands and just bursts out into tears.

"Naina… I… I don't know. I didn't have an idea Sulochana was plotting all this. All this just happened so soon."

"Dumbo…. when will you learn to say right from wrong? And in that big college, people will just make a fool out of you."

Even the thought of leaving my present college sends shudders through me.

We both come out drying our tears, trying to get a hold of us. Sarika Ma'am, being my senior from my department, handles the duty of relieving me. As tough as it is for me, Sarika Ma'am is making it tougher. Clearing my belongings from the almirah- I had got after much ado- I realize it is my last day in this college. It HURTS!

After relieving formalities, they arrange a farewell party for me. *Samosas*[15] and *Gulab jamuns*[16] have arrived. None of the food enthusiasts in my gang are at all enthusiastic today about eating. I know what's going on inside their heads right now- how to turn the tables. However hard they may rack their brains; no idea is going to work out today. It's already late. My resignation, along with every reminiscence of my existence at this place, is handed over to me. There is no going back now.

You can't eat your cake and have it too. To start a new journey, you need to let go of the old one. You can't have it all.

After the *samosa*[15] party, MD Sir and Principal Sir say a few words in my praise. I can notice Teddy Bear's voice is heavy with emotions. I was like a daughter to him, known for respecting elders.

It's all over now. We are ready to mount the bus. It's going to be my last ride on this bus. My throat feels parched with longing. My knees wobble as I drag them to board bus No. 4 for one last time. As I am the last one to enter the bus, the only seat available is beside Mr. Mittal. He gets up and exchanges seats with Naina, who deliberately avoids me. I slump in my seat, and all remain silent for the rest of the journey except Ms. Sarika, who is all chirpy today. She is not in a condition to be able to hold her emotions.

*Oh, God! How much this lady hates me, and how much I hate hatred!*

I make a mental note not to learn to hate; even those who despise me. Because in hating anyone- even the haters–the person burns himself/herself. So, I wish peace even for my rivals and sworn enemies, wishing peace for myself in the bargain.

# 5

# LIFE @ IITM

It is my seventh day at IITM, the college where I still feel like an alien, an outsider, the odd one out; an Assistant Professor in Communication Skills in English in an engineering college. The way all faculty and students treat me here, I feel illiterate.

Honestly, I feel this! I mean, they have no respect for a person from an Arts background.

Just yesterday a student asked me, "Ma'am, if you have done neither commerce nor science, then what have you done?"

I just smiled and explained the following quote from Jonathan Swift to them in that lecture.

'Like the ever–laughing sage, in a jest, I spend my rage (Though let it be understood, I would hang them if I could).'

My batch mates who are from the Arts Stream now seem like the finest individuals on Mother Planet to me. For a few days, I wept after reaching home. I desired to leave that place. But after crying for days and leaving no stone unturned in trying to get back to my previous and much inferior position, now I have decided to prove my mettle in this college.

The fact is, 'the grapes are sour!' And I have no choice left but to carve a niche for myself in IITM.

Bingo! I am ready! And here I am at the college reception waiting for some Ruhaan Sir from the Mechanical Department to join me to perform this Proctorial Duty, an additional duty assigned by our dear HOD, Sarita Ma'am. She has designed this duty where two of the faculty members would loiter around the college campus in turns to make sure that the students don't loiter around; playing truant.

So, while I am waiting for this Ruhaan Sir, the receptionist, an amiable lady in her mid-thirties, admires my hair. "Do you die your hair?" she asks.

"No........." I answer, startled. "No need yet."

"No.... no, I didn't mean that. You're young. But the colour of your hair is jet black. It doesn't look natural, that's why......" Ms. Niharika is all apologetic.

"Yeah, my hair is the only asset as far as beauty is concerned." I act nonchalant.

I excuse myself to go to the washroom that's just opposite the reception

As I come back to the reception enquiring about Ruhaan Sir, Ms Niharika informs me that Ruhaan Sir came when I was in the washroom. And he has just left for the Second Block. "Run, you'll catch him," Ms Niharika suggests.

And I do run. There is no way I am going to perform this duty alone. But how am I going to recognize him? I have never seen him.

I stop a student. "Wait, have you seen Ruhaan Sir?" I ask him.

"Yes, ma'am why?" The boy looks quite gutsy.

"I have work," I retort.

"Ma'am, you can tell me." *Why is he grinning?*

"Why would I tell you? And why are you loitering around? Don't you have class?" I feign anger.

The young man remains calm as earlier, wearing the same sweet smile I love to date.

"I'm Ruhaan, ma'am, and how can I help?" he says and I want the earth to open up and swallow me.

"Ummm.... I mean, you seem to be a student." I gulp the phlegm formed at the back of my throat and mentally slap myself for blabbering this.

"Yeah, even I would have misunderstood you for a student if you hadn't reproached me."

*How sweet of him, and his smile. Why does there seem to be a halo around his head? Am I imagining things? Is he ethereal? Should I touch him to check?*

"I'm sorry," I swallow again as I speak. "I'm Rhythima from the Humanities and Applied Sciences Department."

"Oh... so you are the one who's on duty with me today. Nice to meet you?" He extends a firm hand, and

I put a limp one in it and we shake hands. I keep on grinning like stupid all the time.

"But ma'am, you are late." So, he is being playful now, and so would I.

"No, you are late. I came 15 minutes back. I had just gone to the restroom when you turned up." I fling my chin in the air; hands crossed over my chest.

"Oh, I'm sorry. Please don't complain to the Director Sir." He folds his hands playfully.

I chuckle.

"Wait ma'am, we've to first put our signature at the reception together," he reminds me of the needful.

"Oh, yeah, let's first do the signature."

"Sir, show the whole college to ma'am. She is new," Ms Niharika puts forth.

"Oh, that's why!" He gives me a side glance.

*My God! My ears are getting crimson in embarrassment.*

"Don't worry Niharika Ma'am, I'll show her the whole college," he promises and keeps the promise, too.

He shows me around all the blocks, the library, and even water coolers.

"So, ma'am, this is water cooler," he says, opening his arms like Shahrukh and I guffaw at his sense of humour.

"Ma'am, could you teach me phonetics? I want to learn to speak good English like you."

"Um…" I again turn red. "Anytime, sir, anytime, I'll teach you." I want to say much more, but my heart is pounding at such a speed that I am all tongue-tied.

Ruhaan Sir has something in him which has made me happy for the first time in this college. The Proctorial Duty I was fearing so much earlier has turned out to be a pleasing one.

I ask him about Sanjeev Sir, the HOD of the Computers Department, and he takes me to his office in the Second Block.

My department is in the First Block and all my classes are as well, so I had never been to the Second Block. I have to meet Sanjay Sir about the Language Lab we are planning to set up, but I was hesitant about going to other blocks. Ruhaan Sir shows me all the blocks, which is like a pleasure ride as he knows all. He makes even the sweepers and peons feel at ease, such is his charm.

The duty is over and we have bid goodbyes.

These days I am quite busy setting up the Language Lab. This is a golden opportunity for me to prove my mettle here and create a niche for myself. The whole day long I keep running upstairs and downstairs and have lost a considerable amount of weight. MD Sir is quite impressed with my spirit and Dr Phillips; the Director Sir has been my support system in this college from the very beginning. While I am becoming a favourite of MD Sir and Director Sir, my colleagues have developed a kind of aversion to me. Many times, I have heard them gossiping about me. The other day Rihana Ma'am was saying,

"What's there in her? She is just a faculty in English and can you believe she is getting more than me?"

So now I know the basic reason for their disgust towards me and the very latest and more powerful is that I've snatched their habitat, the Net Lab, where they used to relax in their free time, playing Solitaire, from them. Their Net Lab is going to be transformed into the Language Lab and they cannot forgive me for this.

♥♥♥

Today is Wednesday and I am on my Proctorial Duty, but this time with Rana Ma'am. We are taking a round of the cafeteria when I spot Ruhaan Sir sitting with 3 others. So, he is not on leave. Then why didn't he turn up for the duty? As if reading my thoughts. Rana Ma'am interrogates,

"Your Ruhaan Sir is here in college only. Why didn't he come for duty? I tell you, all these *Mechanchis*[17] are the same; always neglecting their duties." It seems the muscular Rana Ma'am is going to lift a much smaller Ruhaan Sir and throw him for neglecting his duties. I shake my head to wave off this vision and just say, "Hun."

Rana Ma'am gives me a sharp, disapproving look. I gulp as I wonder. During the first two duties, he was quite fine. In fact, friendly; way too friendly. But he stopped coming for Proctorial Duty. He doesn't seem the type who would neglect his duties. Strange, why didn't he come? *Is my gut feeling right? Is he trying to avoid me?* Sure, he is behaving strangely, but *why?* Something is amiss here.

I am about to enter my home after coming back from college when my phone buzzes. It is some unknown number, but when I pick up the phone, the voice seems quite familiar.

"Oh, Ruhaan Sir. Why didn't you show up for the Proctorial Duty today?" The words almost fall from my mouth. *Why is my voice more offended than curious?* He just ignores my question, asking me to check his grammar. He wants me to check the grammatical mistakes in some form he has filled. There are two main sections he wants to be checked for correction. One is, 'Where do you want to see yourself after five years?' against which he has filled 'As Managing Director of the NTPC of top class', and the second is, 'What is your utmost passion?' His answer is, 'I want to uplift some exploited life.' I do the correction by changing the 'exploited' with 'underprivileged'.

♥♥♥

**Next Day**

I am on my way to take my class when Ruhaan Sir approaches me with a weird question. We have had just two meetings and one telephone conversation and here he is asking me,

"Ma'am, would you like to have a cup of tea with me?" My jaw is about to drop when he adds, "It's a kind of farewell. I'm leaving college."

*What!*

*Oh My God, why does it feel awful that he is leaving college? He is not my friend, he is nothing, but I feel almost like*

*crying. Why am I tongue-tied? Why aren't I congratulating him?*

At around 3 pm, I go to the cafeteria for the farewell party. Almost all the lady's staff of the college has shown up. Point to be noted, there is not a single male faculty. Sitting encircled by all the *Gopis*$_{18}$ of IITM, Ruhaan Sir is looking like a *Kanha*$_{19}$. Only if he had worn *mor pankh*$_{20}$ in his hair and had had a flute in his hands, the picture would have been perfect. *Stop this daydreaming, Rhythima,* I mentally smack myself.

On his right side is sitting Priya Ma'am, the most happening faculty of the college. The way they are talking and sitting shoulder to shoulder, they seem intimate. I feel a fish out of water as I search for a seat. Ruhaan Sir, who happens to look at me while others are busy blabbering, gestures to the only unoccupied chair by his side. I slump in the chair, shoulders drooped, hands pressed in my lap, feeling like a complete alien.

*God, why did I come?*

All are in a gala mood. Neha Ma'am gives a long speech on how Mechanical Engineers are mechanics which Ruhaan Sir records to keep as a memory. Everybody has something funny to say about him, which he takes with grace and a smiling face while Priya Ma'am looks like the boss. She is looking after everything from snacks to who should share cold- drinks with whom and why.

When Ruhaan Sir orders two cokes, she cuts him with, "No, only one."

"But why? You too will take coke, won't you?" Ruhaan Sir tries to reason like a kid.

"Yeah, but I know you will not drink the complete bottle, Ruh. So, we will share; why waste money?" The coquettish Priya Ma'am rolls her eyes.

She commands and Ruhaan Sir obeys like an obedient child with his same childlike smile.

*Wait! What did she just call him, Ruh? Something is cooking up here.*

# 6

# The End-a New Beginning

On 25$^{th}$ June 2009, Ruhaan Sir left college to pursue an M. Tech from India's most prestigious institute, IIT Delhi. He was not my friend, just an acquaintance, but there was something in him that made me feel we knew each other in some tacit way. The way he put me at ease, and his eyes beamed with some in-depth knowledge of me, made me comfortable in his company. I would remember that guy as a sweet part of my life.

Now I have gotten busy with my job. Somehow, I have managed to create a niche for myself in IITM. In my spare time, when there is no lab, I teach my colleagues English in the same lab and they are happy with the arrangement. It's Phillips Sir's idea who is going nuts with his typical Haryanvi-speaking faculty. He wants me to polish their eloquence skills, and I'm doing it more than happily. With this, they've accepted me in their work life and don't think of me as lowly a person as they used to.

To an extent, IITM is transforming into a kind of SITE for me, promising more growth and money.

In the evening, I am about to enter my home when my phone buzzes. It's Ruhaan Sir.

*Why does he always call me when I am opening the gate of my house to enter it? Does he know at this time I am free and alone in my house? And how much I have hated it all these years.*

"Hello, IITian sir," I greet him.

"Not yet, *Dilli abhi duur hai*[21]. There is still one month."

"Then why did you leave college so early? After all, we had just met?"

*What happens to my tongue when I talk to this guy?* It seems out of control.

"Oh ma'am, if I had known you were going to join, I would not have applied for resignation."

I bit my lower lip, realising it's going too far. I try to change the topic.

"You are a sham. Today I saw your Orkut profile and I cannot help being surprised that you have a girlfriend. I had an altogether different idea about you."

"Thank you, ma'am. Huh… but by the way, what does sham mean?"

"It means a pretender who pretends to be what he is not; you are a *chaalu*[22]."

"Oh…. thank you, thank you. Thank you so much for giving me this title."

"I never had the slightest idea that you are such a sort of guy; I always thought that you are a mama's boy and a studious chap."

"Please don't call me that, ma'am," comes the quick reply.

"Tell me, do you drink?"

"Why are you so surprised ma'am, it's a normal thing, cool you know?"

*Cool!*

Getting worried, I respond, "Don't tell me you are addicted to drinking."

"Yes, ma'am, it's a truth."

"Now you are trying to fool me."

*Wait, why am I getting concerned, like really concerned? Am I his mother or what?*

"*Arre*[23] madam, why would I befool you? I began drinking long before I began smoking."

"Now it's too much. I know you are not that sort of boy; you are a nice boy." *Why Rhythima why; why in the name of God are you concerned?*

"Ma'am, what makes you think so? I drink regularly and I am a chain smoker."

"Oh, my God!" I slap my forehead, asking, "Does your girlfriend know this?"

"Oh, ma'am, she is the only one responsible for teaching me all this. She has made me addicted to drugs."

"Now it's a white lie. It cannot be true."

*Did I just snort?*

"Come on, ma'am, what do you think? Girls don't drink."

"From where is your girlfriend?"

"She is from Delhi."

"Then it may be true, but how can you like such a girl?" My heart is sinking now. *Is he that spoiled?*

"I like her only for this quality."

"Oh, my God! You are just impossible, you........... I don't know what to say."

"This is my quality, ma'am."

"I know you are telling lies; you can't be an alcoholic."

"Come on, ma'am, why are you so much surprised? It's a normal thing for me. My father has taken me to the rehabilitation centre so many times, but I'm addicted."

"I could never think so about you, even in my worst dream. You are either trying to make a fool out of me or you are a *chaalu*[22] number one, a sham."

"Thank you very much, ma'am, for giving me this title."

"Oh, you are just impossible, having a girlfriend who drinks?"

"Ma'am, for your kind information, she takes drugs as well. She cannot stand on her own. She is not even in a condition to take *phere*[24]."

"Oh, my God! And there I was going all spiritual about you thinking such a pure guy, imagining a halo around your head, all this while writing poems…"

*O teri ki*[25]… *What did I blurt out?* I bite my tongue.

"What… what did you just say? You wrote poems for me."

*Relax Rhythima, the cat is out of the bag now, so better you confess it.*

"Relax, don't be too excited. I wrote just one poem, and it is not some love song. Um…. see, this is the thing with me… err… that poems just happen to me. I don't write them on purpose. Sometimes they come and knock… yes… knock and keep knocking and that also so hard that I cannot have peace till I write those lines."

"That sounds interesting!" He is all excited now as he complains, "And you never told me. I want that poem."

"It's of no use now. I wrote it for a different person, but now as you are not that person with the spiritual aura or halo…"

"No… no, I am that very person you thought me to be," he cuts in.

"Then what was all that you just said about smoking, drinking and all?"

"Um… I was just…"

*I know you want to belittle yourself in my eyes, but why? Why do you want to prove yourself to be some notorious person?* I want to yell but check my tongue.

He says he is coming to college for one last time to settle his dues and wants that poem. So, we agree to meet at IITM for one last time.

# 7

# We Meet @ IITM

After being done with all the formalities, he comes to my cubicle. He is all jubilant with his smile but not the usual one that always graces his face. Today it's not a grin, but a genuine heartfelt smile that starts somewhere behind his throat and reaches his eyes, making them shine. I still can see that halo around his head. I smack my forehead to shake off the enchantment of temple bells ringing and the flute playing, and greet him. He gesticulates with his hands, his eyes, and the whole of his body, including even his nose, to show him the poem. I extend my hand to give him the motivational book I had bought at some fair with the poem inside it.

Ruhaan sir you are really the Conqueror of heart

Because wherever you go your spell you always cast

With your sweet -sweet smile and pure and lovely heart

In fact, your purity is your grace

Every thought of yours always brings smile on my face

Although whatever and whenever I did that was all nonsense talk

But that feeling I always had that you have got some special spark

Whenever I teach phonetics to someone how much I wish

That genius were in my class

Who always wanted to learn it but could never start

Whenever you become a Managing Director of an NTPC of top class

(As I've full faith, you will be)

Just remember there's one person a small part of your history

Who's celebrating it as her own victory

Now as you will be a part of materialistic strife

Don't forget you have also to uplift one underprivileged life

And remember to always keep your humanity alive

And thanks for being a part of life of mine

I'll always stay indebted to thine

For teaching me some of your arts

You'll always stay nearby my heart

With the hope we'll meet again and I'll have some sensible talk

With a person who's so great at so young an age
I'll stop.

For the first time in my life, I ask a person to write a few lines for me. And here is what he wrote for me.

Dear Rhythima Ma'am

Actually, I am very weak in English, you already know that. Also, my tenses, grammar & punctuation are having a large no. of mistakes. That's why I cannot write a lot about you although I want to write a lot.

Better If I were Shakespeare, I would have written a large no. of poems on you.

You say you are boring but you have a very jolly nature. You are an excellent person. You are one of the nicest girls I have ever seen in my life.

I am a big fan of your voice. Your voice is simply excellent.

I would like to be in touch with you always.

You can call me anytime.

Wish you all the best and wish you a very happy and prosperous future.

Ruhaan

July 01, 2009

*What's happening here? Why my heart is jumping on reading these lines?*

He's long gone, and I had to struggle a lot to understand his 't's'. I have read that paper almost a hundred times, especially the parts that are underlined. *Am I going mad?*

No one, literally no one, except my teachers, of course, has ever praised me in my entire life. My family, of course not, no matter how hard I try to make a place in their lives. Except for babysitting and doing household chores, I have no place there.

*God, this is the right moment! Take my breath right away. This is the right moment. My birth on this earth is successful.*

It was my last meeting with him, according to me, but God is a great planner. He never let us know what is there in his book next for us. When we think it is the end, it comes out to be a new beginning. I did not have the slightest idea that I would receive a call from him the very day, which I thought to be the last day of my meeting with him.

He calls me in the evening at the same time when I am about to enter my home. My phone buzzes and my heart just hops on seeing his name flashing on the screen of my phone. He says he has never felt this way in his life before.

"I will never forget it. I'll remember it even after a hundred years," he says in a tone which sounds the most honest in this world.

He asks me to call him whenever I feel like it and informs me that he is leaving for Delhi on the 24th of July. I am all numb, my mind registering nothing.

Generally, people face the problem of being uncomfortable with others, but my problem is that of being uncomfortable with myself. But I don't know what is there in him that I feel comfortable and light with him. Even his thought brings a smile to my face. I know, for him, I am an ordinary girl, just one of his acquaintances whom he can easily forget. But for me, he is, if not an angel, a person who has changed my life, and who will linger in my thoughts for long. In him sometimes I see my papa. But I cannot share these thoughts with him, neither do I want to. In his company, I feel I am a small kid again, sitting in my father's lap, safe and secure, with no fear of judgment or being looked down upon.

*What a strange feeling this is, but I am loving it!*

# 8

# Bhaiya's Engagement

**24/7/2009**

I have got some exciting news today. My brother is going to get engaged, yippee! His ring ceremony is just tomorrow and I am making calls to my dear ones to invite them for the big day. It's not that I have come to know about it just today. But you know I.... I kept putting it off till I could. I was busy too. OK, not that busy. I am a procrastinator. I admit.

The first one on my list, of course, is Naina. With a sinking heart and trembling hands, I punch her number. I haven't called her in ages and whenever she called; I was busy proving my mettle. For that, I am going to get a good lashing from her. I gulp as soon as I ring her, making up some excuses in my mind. On the third ring, the tigress picks up. But wait, she has not pounced upon me. Rather, she is all goofy. And there is an additional chuckle in her Uncle Scrooge's voice when she asks me,

"Who's he?"

"W...Who's who?" I stammer.

"He who makes you blush," she chuckles.

"What?"

*By the way, am I blushing?*

"Now don't say there's no one."

"Naina."

"So, should I talk to Mittal? He is still waiting."

"Naina."

"Oh, ho… so we have got a new Rhythima all blushing and shying… Won't you kill me for teasing you in the name of Mittal?" Her laughter echoes.

"Naina, stop all this nonsense."

"Um…" She takes a deep sigh. "You are a big gun now; we will seem only nonsense to you."

"Stop this melodrama and listen to me."

"No, you listen first," she cuts in. "Be expressive… tell him… he's the one for you."

*What is this Lady Gaga blabbering about?*

"Naina, you know me. No boys, only career in my dictionary."

"Tell him," Naina insists.

*Oh… such an adamant devil.*

"Okay, cut the crap…. *bhaiya*[4] is getting engaged tomorrow. So, you have got to be here."

As I expected, now she reprimands me for telling her so late. *God, save me!*

Almost all the calls are done. I am in a dilemma about whether to call him when I receive a message and my heart, in the genuine sense of the word, skips a couple of beats.

'You have a very special place in my life. I am just a call away from you. Whenever you miss me, call me.'

*Why am I not able to breathe?* Blood is pounding in my ears. I double-check to confirm, is it for me?

Such a message wouldn't have meant a thing to any other girl. But to me, it is a treasure.

When nice things come to you of their own, without you asking for them, without your least expecting them, you feel over the moon. And to be of some value to someone, to be desired, is one such thing. Who knows better than me what it means to be desired, to be of use, to be of value, to not to be unwanted?

I am trying to come out of this shock when another bolt follows.

'As I'm leading towards a new life, just want to thank you for making my life worth living. Thanks for being a part of my life.

*Always Yours*

*Sham'*

Oh, My God, I will die of happiness. God, kill me right now, in this very moment with at least one person in my life to whom I mean something apart from babysitting or doing household chores. *God, am I hallucinating things?* I have heard that when there is a dearth of love and there is loneliness, people imagine things to fill that void. *Am I doing the same? Am I hallucinating?*

I double-check the messages to confirm my sanity. And it is confirmed as my phone buzzes. It's Ruhaan Sir calling. I am in a state of a daze. All I can manage to say is,

"It's my brother's ring ceremony tomorrow."

He answers he has reached Delhi and has called me to give me his new number.

# 9

# AND THE FRIENDSHIP BEGINS

*Bhaiya*[4] has got engaged and I am going to get a *bhabhi*[26] soon. I am so thrilled.

I am a little disheartened, though. *Bhabhi*[26] seems shy. Whenever I try, she doesn't talk. I keep pestering *bhaiya*[4] to call her. *Are arranged marriages boring?*

One more news. Naina has shifted to Chandigarh. She has got a job there and is living with her *mama*[27]. She comes to her home on weekends. She sounds happier now. I am happy for her, but my heart cries. It's been long since I met her. And my gang from college has got distant. We were 8 friends; each of us having some unique talent. One was a singer, one dancer, one interior decorator, one fashion designer, one good orator, and me, the writer. How we used to make plans that we'd stay together and today, we're not even in touch. Some have got married and some are busy working. But all are far away.

Sham, aka Ruhaan, has never called me after going to IIT. Even I am determined not to call him. But today, I am just about to cry. Nobody is home. Some distant relative of would-be *bhabhi*[26] has passed away. *Bhaiya*[4] and Mom have gone there and won't be back till morning. Naina can't talk, she is with her monster, sorry mother and brother.

I am contemplating whether I should call Ruhaan Sir or not. *What if he has forgotten all about me?* I'll make a fool out of myself. But it was he who gave me his Delhi number. I contest in my heart for about fifteen minutes and finally give in.

"Hello, who's there?" a tired voice talks into the phone.

Oh, my heart breaks. *He is not even having my number saved, and I am dying after him.*

"H.... hello, Rhythima from IITM." Tears have already pooled in my eyes.

"Oh, Rhythima Ma'am, how are you? I've formatted my phone. That's why I have no contacts, *Aur Sunaiye*[28]."

OH! My heart relaxes a bit. But sensing he is quite busy; I plan to make up an excuse for calling.

"Sir, needed some help." There is an awkward pause as I clumsily search for the right words.

"Ma'am, please order."

*Oh... Why is his voice so pleasing and soothing to my ears?*

"MD Sir has asked all the faculty members to give the names of companies where we can get the students placed, but I have no such contacts," my excuse to call is ready.

"Oh...... don't worry, ma'am, I know one or two such people who can help you."

After getting the required information, I enquire about his studies, but he sounds low.

"Life is tough here. I feel pressurized," he says with a weary sigh.

"Hey, you are a champ, you'll do. Remember my poem, you have got a special spark."

He gets happy on hearing this, but has to hang up as his mother is calling.

I realize things have changed for him; he has no time for my chit-chat so I decide not to bother him with my casual calls again.

♥♥♥

**Next Day**

It's Monika's wedding today. Remember Monika, our cute little receptionist at SITE? I am meeting my *Chandal-Chaukdi*[2] after such a long time. I may have created that niche for myself at IITM, but nothing can beat the feeling of being with my gang. All are the same, Shravan Sir delivering his food *gyaan*[12], Tanmay *bhaiya*[4] running errands, and Naina teasing me. Thank God, Mittal Sir could not make it. He has gone bride-hunting. I can't help but laugh as Dhingra Sir tells us about his preferences for a girl. Whichever family he goes to meet; he calls it an envelope. He is looking for girls who can fit into his envelope and one of his requirements from the girl is an hour-glass figure. And he is bride-hunting the same way as he rides a bike, with no breaks and at full speed. Even if a person comes into his way, he has no habit of using breaks or slowing down. That's why I named him accelerator-*toofani*[1]. He is an accelerator-*toofani*[1] even while bride-hunting. My God! I can't even stand his thought.

All are busy in their general blabbering when Naina nudges me, throwing me obscene grins.

"Naina…, has Mittal assigned you the duty to play his role today?" I demand.

"Ummm…" she clears her throat to begin her nonsense. "No, I just want to tell you, you're blooming. Look at yourself, you were never this beautiful. He indeed is making you beautiful and also easy to deal with." Naina smiles, a hint of amusement in her eyes.

"I'm a broken person, Naina. And to pick my pieces is not his responsibility."

"Have you ever heard of Kintsugi, the Japanese art of repairing broken objects with gold, creating something more beautiful through the acts of breaking and repair? He's doing the same to you, making you more beautiful."

"How can you be so sure he loves me? You've not even seen him," I challenge her judgment.

Naina's lips spread in a chuckle as she says, "I've seen you. In the curl of your lips, the sparkle in your eyes, the tint of blush on your cheeks, he is everywhere, Rhythima. It's visible to everyone except you. You are blossoming. Don't let this slip away; just Let Love Happen."

"Love is not for me, Naina, you know it," I respond.

"Protect yourself from this world's bitterness, and soak yourself in the love you are lucky to get," Naina almost begs.

I'm about to retort when my phone buzzes.

I look at Naina, trying to make an excuse. And here goes our Emma the Great, "Take it. I know it's him. Look at the glow on your face."

I just roll my eyes and excuse myself.

"Hello, are you all right?" I speak into the phone as I scuttle away.

"Yeah, I'm great," says he in a heavy voice.

"Hey, don't lie. Tell me why you are crying."

"Nothing."

"Come on, speak up, and calling at this time. Haven't you gone for your tuition?" I know he has joined coaching to prepare for the IES Exam.

"It's too difficult to survive here in the IIT and then coaching, I'm not able to keep pace, I……. I must die."

"What's the matter? Please tell me."

"I've failed all the house tests. If it happens in finals, I won't even get the scholarship. How am I going to pay my fees?" His throat is choked.

"Oh, that's the matter. First, wipe your tears and sit on your bed."

"Yeah. My father is right. I'm good for nothing," he mumbles.

"What Yeah? Wipe off your tears and sit on the bed. Look, I know it's very tough over there in the IIT and very easy for me to sermonize on the phone. But listen, you are one of those students who are considered the cream of India. You have reached the IIT after cracking the toughest exam. You competed with the brightest students; you did it once, you will do it again. And listen, you've failed the house tests, not the final exams. And please don't prove your father right. Don't even think of taking any wrong step, *ullu*[29]."

This brings a smile to his face. I can sense all his emotions even while sitting 160 km away from him.

"Now stop grinning."

"How do you know?" asks he, his smile broadening even more.

"You know I can read you, even your silence."

"How? Are you an astrologer?"

"Now come on, get up, wash your face and start preparing for exams. I need a daily report."

"Yes, ma'am," says he filled with a new energy

He is like *Hanuman Ji*[30]; every time needs to be told what he is.

♥♥♥

His final exams have begun. I am more tense than him. I call him daily to get daily report of his preparation and he is doing wonders. Every day, I send him some motivational quote, and after the exam, he calls me telling me how great his paper has gone.

"I wish I could show you my papers, Motto." By now he has given me a name, Motto. I must have been the only girl in this world who enjoys being called Motto, which means fat, though I am quite slim.

"See, I told you, everything would be fine. And all this fret and worry is just for two years. Once it's over, you will come out as a great person. Your parents will be proud of you."

"Yes."

"What, now why that naughty smile on your face?" I playfully scold, settling my palm under my chin while lounging on the bed, lying flat on my stomach.

"How do you know that I'm smiling?" his voice is husky as he speaks.

"You know I know you better than you."

"Then you must know why that smile."

*Why is his voice getting huskier every moment?*

"Now, I'm not an astrologer."

"You know, talking to you has become as essential a thing as doing brush," he nearly whispers in my ear.

"So, my importance is equal to that of a brush, happy to know." I exhale a fake melancholic sigh.

"Um……."

"Now what?"

"Could I tell you everything about me?"

"Yes, of course." I am elated. Being of use always gives me happiness.

"I've one more problem."

"Tell me, I'll solve it. Why fear when Rhythima is here?" I declare in a sing-song voice.

"I get... physically… attracted."

*What the…* I get up with a jerk from the bed.

*Why in the world is he discussing this with me?*

"Um... My friend Risha is an expert on this. You must talk to her," I manage to speak on the phone, plopping on the bed again, still panting with horror.

Getting embarrassed at the same time realizing my discomfort, he hangs on the pretext he has to go for coaching.

*What was that, man?*

Neither of us has ever brought out the last conversation about his being attracted and things are going well. Within these couple of weeks, our friendship has become very strong; talking to him is as important as doing brush, what an analogy! Do dreams come true and God listens to prayers? Only two weeks back I had kept fasts asking God for, guess what, a friend.

'Please, God, give me a friend who understands me and fills my loneliness or give me a husband who's like a friend. No matter if the friend is a girl or boy or uncle or aunty, just he/she understands me!'

Look how clever I am in my prayers, either a friend or husband. And God has listened so early. Two weeks into fasting, and He has provided me with a friend. Whenever I talk to him on the phone, I wonder if it is *Sai*[31] I am talking to as I have never had such a person in my life who made me feel so happy and made my life worth living. All these days, my faith in *Sai*[31] has grown so much stronger that I have almost begun to believe that it is *Sai*[31] I am talking to.

# 10

## The First Date

I have come shopping with my mother in Karnal for my brother's wedding. We have done most of the shopping and are just making payments when he calls. He is at the Kurukshetra University. I cannot talk much as I am with Mom. But I have a feeling that he wants to meet me. While on the bus, an idea strikes me. I could head to the University under the pretext of getting some books from the library. Informing my mother, I call him upon reaching Pipli, to check whether the library is open. He takes 45 minutes to confirm. The truth is, I need no books, nor was he in the University when I called him; we both were making a plot to meet.

Exiting the auto, I make my way to the library. It will take me fifteen minutes to reach the University Library. So many emotions are pounding in my heart. The anticipation and a continuous grin accompany me as I remember our recent telephone conversation.

*"Hun, look at yourself, you Amitabh Bachchan*[32]*. I'm taller than you."*

*"Really?" he replied without objecting, as is his habit.*

As I approach the library, I spot him standing in the parking zone with his scooter. A mischievous smile plays on his face.

"Why that naughty smile on your face?" I enquire as I reach him.

"No, just admiring your height, you are indeed taller," he says, the naughty smile now triumphant.

"Oh… that." *My God, these days I turn red so soon.* "OK, I agree you are taller, but not very much. Boys are generally taller, but I prefer 6-foot-tall boys." I pout.

"Oh, really?" says he this time with a naughtier grin.

This is our first meeting after he went to IIT. As he is not very familiar with the University, I take him to the English Department, my English Department, where I spent two pleasant years of my life studying Literature. Little did I know it would become our regular meeting spot, witnessing our fights, promises, kisses and more.

*Why is my heart doing Zumba on meeting him?* I seem to be on auto-pilot mode.

On reaching the first floor, we settle on the stairs in front of the room for the previous year's students. I return him the slam book he had given me to fill during our last meeting at IITM. As he opens it to read, he gets annoyed. In the birth date section, I have written 'on … December this curse fell on earth'. This is the reason for his annoyance. *Oh, God, this person makes me feel so special. Is he sent by You to be my real friend?*

To enlighten his mood and break the ice, I ask what are Chemical Engineers.

"It's a great career choice, very promising," he says, curious. "But why are you asking?"

"A proposal has come for me; mother is ready."

"Wow, great Rhythima Ma'am! I'm so happy for you. Chemical Engineering is a great career choice." He starts singing songs in praise of that guy as if he were hands and gloves with him.

"But I'm afraid to get married. I don't want to."

*Why is it so that I can share my deepest fears and darkest of secrets with him? Oh God, is it really You? If so, please guide me should I marry that Chemical Engineer guy or not.*

"These are just fears," he announces, breaking my reverie. "Once you get to know the guy, you'll feel for him. Yeah, remember, talk a lot to him on the phone so that you both can understand each other and develop a liking for each other. He must be earning great."

"Money is not a matter with me. It's just that I can't marry anyone. I've seen my cousin married to a guy she doesn't love. I can't do this, just not."

"Hey, these are just fears," he reassures.

"No, I'm not a normal girl. Who'd like me? Who'd love me…"

"Why not?"

"I can't live in a relationship without love."

"OK, just do one thing, compare that guy to your father, if he……."

I get blank at the mention of the word father. Saying, "Papa……." I get choked. Tears stream down my cheeks. As he sees me crying, sitting on the third last stair while he is sitting on the stair above me, he gets restless, as if he has done something wrong. As I am immersed in tears, I don't know what comes over him; he comes to me, gives me a peck on the right cheek and the next moment he is sitting on the last stair with his head dropped fearing as if he has committed some crime. It all happened so suddenly and instantaneously that we both could not make out what was it. A moment back I was talking to him about my fears of marriage, who'll love me and so on and so forth and suddenly that strange thing happened leaving us both speechless. But there seems nothing wrong with that kiss to me. It felt like a warm hand on my troubled heart, which hasn't recovered from the shock of my father's demise. I was just 12 at that time. I feel I am that small bubbly girl again, sitting with my father, embraced in his love and warmth of security.

We are sitting like this in sheer silence when he takes out a notebook from his backpack and, tearing off a piece of paper, starts writing on it. Every word he has written feels like balm on my troubled soul that has lived in the inferiority complex all these years.

Dear Rhythima,

You have one problem, and that is you underestimate yourself. The truth is that you are the most-most-most loving and beautiful girl in this world. Yes, The MOST BEAUTIFUL AND LOVING GIRL IN THIS COMPLETE WORLD. I really don't know why you consider yourself a curse. Maybe you are suffering from the same problem as me. The problem of underestimating oneself. That Chemical Engineer must have done some really good deeds or, in other words, you can say must have donated the pearls in his previous life. Rhythima anybody-literally anybody who will come in touch with you will love you. Yes, he will definitely love you.

And the thing is the day when you enter his life would be the best day of his life. And the persons you reject are losers in life. It's their bad luck. Never think that nobody will love you. The thing is, you are like a rose whose fragrance everyone will like to make his. Really. Sorry for the grammatical errors & mistakes. They have been made intentionally to check your English knowledge.

Thanks

Ruhaan

18 July 2010

I once again enter my auto-pilot mode on reading the lines and give him a poem I had written on friendship.

When we climb down the stairs to part, he invites me to sit on his scooter. We both are a little hesitant; he is because he does not have a bike, and I am because I have never sat behind a boy except my brother earlier. I sit behind him. We both head towards the auto stand. We both are silent, but this is not some disturbing silence. We are feeling relieved.

The world looks so beautiful suddenly and my reverence for *Sai*[31] gets tenfold.

Again, I read every alphabet a hundred times after coming home, this time without struggling with his 't's'.

# 11

# THE PROPOSAL

**19/07/2010**

It's a holiday. My *buas*[33] have gathered at home, indulging in their usual banter. I feel a strong urge to escape as they discuss Papa. Why can't they be sensitive enough to see how sensitive I am? My heart is on the verge of tearing off, and I need an excuse to leave. Thankfully, my phone buzzes, granting me the perfect opportunity. Now I can make an excuse. I grab my phone and climb the stairs to my brother's room.

As I say hello on the phone, a low voice speaks, "I'm worthless."

"Why would you say that? Today is a day to celebrate. You secured the third rank in IIT, a nine-pointer! Even Chetan Bhagat was only a five-pointer."

"Now, how do you know that?" He sounds despondent.

"Ever heard of his book, 'Five Point Someone'?"

"But how do you know he is a five-pointer?"

"Leave that. Tell me why are you so low despite your remarkable achievement."

"Nothing. You tell me how is college?"

"Oh… so you don't want to tell me?"

"In front of all - *bua*[33], *dadi*[34], *chachaji*[35], my father declared today that I'm good for nothing." He has been crying all this while, trying to hide from me. *But doesn't he know I can read him?*

Trying to uplift his spirits, I reply, "Hey…. Come on, stop behaving like a kid. Your father might have said this in anger. He must be mad at you for something. Some people don't know how to express their concern and love and behave in strange ways."

"Hope, you're right."

"Now, when are you treating me?" I attempt to shift the conversation.

"Anytime, you tell."

"On Sunday, the first of August."

"OK done. Now it's your turn," he jests.

"My turn, for what?"

"To talk."

"About what?"

"To share why you are feeling so low."

"No, I'm fine," I respond, trying to sound upbeat.

"Hey……… I know you can read me better, but even I can do it to some extent. Won't you tell me?"

"Not any serious matter. You know, it's summer vacation. All my *buas*[33] have gathered at home and they were discussing Papa." I get choked. *I feel someday I will die of choking!*

He knows how horrible I get at the mention of my father. And I know he can do anything to cheer up my mood.

"You know something? I'm going to miss you a lot," I murmur, the words tapering off. I want to tell him that with him I feel as I used to feel around my father. He really can change my mood even though it means dropping a bombshell on my head. Next, he is going to do only that.

"Hey Rhythima, there is something I haven't told you. I don't know if I should tell you or not, but there's something," he sounds mysterious.

"What?" Now I am all curious.

"You remember Prakash Sir in the Mechanical Department?"

"Y… Yes!"

"Once he came to me with a proposal of marriage."

"Hun."

"The girl was you."

"W…. what are you saying? Not possible… not just possible." *Will my eyes pop out of my head?*

"It's true?"

"How… I mean no, not possible. How Old Are You? I mean, are you even of marriageable age?"

"For your kind information, I am an adult." He gets offended.

"I didn't mean that; I mean, you are quite young. I bet you are much younger than I. I am 26. How old are you?"

"I am 23. But how does Prakash Sir know your age? And you know what? I missed a golden opportunity, *yaar*[36]. If I had known what you are, I'd never have missed such a golden opportunity."

"That's not funny."

"Hey... I'm serious."

"So, you would have said yes?"

"Why not? There is no reason to say no."

"You are kidding."

"No Motto. But then our relationship would not have been the same as it is today."

"Oh my God, what are you saying? I can't even think about it; I am so much older than you."

I try imagining myself as his bride. *No… that's sacrilege!*

"I've missed a golden opportunity. Now there's no hope. Yes, one hope is there. I can wait for Prakash Sir's proposal," he sounds desperate.

"OK, if you get a proposal again, what would you do?" I challenge.

"I'll say yes."

"Is it possible?" *Have I heard it right?*

"I like you." The three words echo in my earlobes as if they echoed in a valley, 'I like you... I like you... I like you.'

"But can you love me?" I raise my brows.

"This word doesn't exist in my dictionary, but I like you."

"But how's it possible? I mean, I like you. I remain happy in your company. I feel comfortable only with you. I always want to keep you with me, but I cannot think about marriage. I mean, I don't like you in that way. And what about society and family members?"

"To hell with society. Does society stand by me during my tough times? I've nothing to do with society. That day when I was planning suicide, it was you who was with me, not society."

"Wait… when did you plan a suicide?" I am worried.

"Leave it, just tell me."

"But I don't deserve you. You can find a far better girl than me."

"OK, what kind of girl deserves me? Tell me."

"One who's beautiful, fair, charming, from some sound family and a doctor or an engineer." My auto-pilot mode is on, and so is his.

"OK, tell me what do you mean by sound family? You mean richer. Now tell me, what will I do with her family's money? It'll be of no use. Secondly, you said beautiful. You are beautiful, very charming, and sweet. And thirdly, a doctor or an engineer. Why does only a doctor or an engineer deserve me? Why not a Professor of Communication Skills? This point is baseless and illogical."

*What has happened to this guy? Give me a break.*

"Wait… wait… wait. There are certain norms our society has set up; we can't break them."

"OK, tell me, you love me or not."

"Of course, I love you, but not in that way. I mean, I have never thought that way about you. I can't, I can't be cheap, and you are so much younger than I am."

"OK……." *What has gotten into him? Why is he so desperate to convince me?*

"I'll ask my *Sai*[31]," I interrupt him.

I cannot sleep. I am just twisting and tossing in my bed. I know my mom is getting irritated. I better stay calm before she throws me out of here. I am thinking, like seriously thinking. Getting him is like getting the universe, but how could I even think of getting him in that way? He is so young. I am no match for him.

♥♥♥

**Next day**

As expected, he calls me. I know him so very well. I know he is tensed but won't say anything at all. So, I break the ice.

"I could not sleep the whole night," I declare.

"I know I've snatched your peace. Rhythima, please do me a favour. I know it's difficult. But try to erase the last day of your life. Just forget whatever I told you, I meant nothing," he pleads.

"Are you all right? Did you sleep?"

"I had a sound sleep. I don't take tension. But I ….."

*He knows very well I can read his silence. Then why is he lying? But God, I can't make him feel guilty. His sad voice makes me sad. I should come back to normal.*

"Hey, I'm all right, absolutely all right," I interrupt, feigning cheerfulness.

I know he cannot see me in pain, either. He is such a pure soul; he cannot see anyone in pain. And trying hard for the sake of each other, we return to our normal mood by and by.

"I love my parents, I love my brother, the same way I love you. There is nothing wrong with it. You are my friend, my best friend. You own a very special place in my life," he concludes.

"And that is what I need," I conclude.

Hurray! Things have returned to normal between us.

❖❖❖

# 12

# The Second Date

After trying hard and taking solemn pledges not to meet again, here we are, facing each other for the second time. It is for the first time that I am wearing a top and denim in his presence. Back in college, he had only seen me in a *salwar kameez*[37]. He raises his eyebrows on seeing me, but I choose to ignore it. Something seems different in his eyes, a hint of mischief. Those once-innocent eyes carry a new aura. As I approach him, he begins clicking my pictures, prompting me to cover my face with a handkerchief. Being a victim of inferiority complex, I have always been camera-conscious.

We don't dare to go upstairs to sit on the stairs of the English Department. We both have changed, our trust in each other shaken after his proposal. Following his impromptu photo session, he discloses a need for help with his English studies. Now what does a blind man need? I agree to assist. I had resolved to stay strong. But he surprises me by revealing a foolproof plan to make me despise him.

Today he admits that he intentionally portrayed himself as notorious in front of me. And the reason for his actions leaves me in shock. The guy believed I loved him and I had sent that proposal of marriage.

*What the... What on earth made him think so?*

I give him a good piece of my mind and laugh at the misunderstanding. I assure him I knew nothing about that proposal while questioning why Prakash Sir, with whom I have no relation, presented him with my proposal.

The revelation that he lived under the impression that I loved him is both shocking and amusing. He shows me photographs featuring almost all the unmarried female faculty of IITM. Some of the images disturb me for reasons unknown. I get up to leave. He follows suit, but there is a sadness looming large on his face. We decide to part, promising never to meet again as our meetings are getting somewhat complicated. There is some sort of tension developing between us, especially on his part. He deliberately tries to sit away from me and never goes inside to sit on the stairs of the English Department. He even tries to avoid looking at me and when he does, his eyes are not the same. *What's wrong?*

I don't know what, but there is something between us. An unknown force seems to bind us, preventing us from severing the invisible knot that exists between us, despite our efforts. I can read him like an open book. I understand why he showed me those photos- mere trickery. I also sense that he is not content with his actions. His emotions are laid bare on his face.

I know he left convinced today that I would not call him again, his heart quietly grieving.

The words he has written for me today speak what he couldn't convey verbally. Along with words, he has brought two books for me, claiming they are from a friend's house. However, I know he purchased them. *Why and how do I know every intricacy of this man, oh God? Why are you making it complicated? I was finally happy to find a friend, so why force us to refrain from meeting? Why his eyes are changing towards me every moment?*

Here are the words he wrote for me:

> Rhythima, when your first article will be published, I will be happier than you. Please don't deprive me of that happiness. Please send me a mail or call me when you get your poems published.
>
> Always remember you are my best friend (I know I don't hold that place in your life. But you will always remain my best friend). I will be just a call away from you. Whenever you need my help, just give me a call. Hardly matters wherever I am, just a call away from you.
>
> Thanks
>
> Friendship Day,
>
> 1 August 2010

# 13

# The Third Date

So, we have decided to remain friends, very good friends, the best of friends.

After deciding we wouldn't talk much to each other, we have started talking even more; it is not just as necessary as brushing, but as going to the loo.

After trying hard not to, we also meet for the third time.

"What is our relationship?" he queries.

"We are best friends," I answer casually, knowing deep down that it means more. What exactly? I have no answer.

"It's strange," he responds. "I have so many friends, but I cannot share the things with them I can with you. You know I don't let even my mother touch my cupboard, but I can show it to you," he says innocently.

Pride swells within me.

"You know, we are not as rich as we give the impression to be. My father's business is not that good. We are just from hand to mouth."

There is such innocence in his talk that he looks like a small, sullen, innocent baby. And I feel proud of being his confidant, his only confidant, as he would say.

"You are so sweet, just like a baby," I cannot stop myself from saying.

"You know what? I don't want to do a job," he starts sharing his secrets, which he has not shared with anyone, with me. I am all ears.

"Then, want to do business?" I probe.

"I don't know, but I don't want to do my father's business either."

"Then what?"

"Maybe business, but not my father's."

"I know what you want."

"What?"

"You want to become a Managing Director and uplift the lives of underprivileged students by helping them, maybe in their studies."

"How do you know?"

"You told me once. Remember when you had to fill out a form, you called me to get the grammar checked, then you told me."

"Yeah……. how did I forget?"

I can sense something amiss in the father and son relationship. But right now, I am more concerned about him than about his relationship with his father. His sweet, innocent face tempts me to take it in my palms and make him believe that I'm always there for him, but I better restrain my emotions.

♥♥♥

Things have changed completely. Nothing can stop me from meeting him. After all, I've got my best friend finally. Mother is getting a little suspicious. But no reason or no hurdle on earth can stop me. However hard my mother tries to stop me, I always come out with a good new reason to go to KUK. I have become a master of making excuses.

OK! Time for some confessions. My behaviour these days is not normal. I know I am getting smitten by his charms. So today I am going to meet him to bid him the final goodbye. He is proving more of an addiction to me.

In the English Department corridor, sitting at our designated places on the stairs, I on the third last stair and he on the stair above me- I state,

"We shouldn't meet."

He remains silent, agreeing. *Why does it hurt?* I can feel a dagger in my heart.

"By the way, what were you doing with all those ma'am's of IITM?" I ask, tears welling up.

"I'm like this. I used to spend evenings with them all. I have photographs of Priya Ma'am in every single attire. How ravishing she looked at the Freshers' Party in that *sari*[38] and sleeveless blouse," he tries to let out a moaning sound while speaking.

"Really?" simmering inside, I question.

"Yes!"

*Why are his eyes glistening? Are there tears in his eyes?*

"See, we know our relationship cannot work out, so we should not stretch it any further." I turn my face to stay strong.

"Hun," he responds in interjections. *Is he choked like me?*

My heart fills with warmth. I don't know what comes over me. I hug him tightly, saying, "It won't be easy to forget you."

As I put my arms around him, I can hear his heart. Dhak… dhak… dhak… dhak; it is beating like a drum. *Oh God, how I want to die in this very moment, in these warm arms, with my ears placed on this lovely heart filled with nothing but love for me.*

Tucking at my shoulders for the first time, he looks into my eyes as if wanting to do something very intimate. Controlling himself, he says,

"You know Motto, I love you. I love you the way no one in this world has loved anybody, but I can't marry you."

The three magical words penetrate through my chest, making a straight way to my heart. I close my eyes, trying to savour these memories for a lifetime. I won't be able to resist myself anymore from declaring my love for him. But I can't do that. I can't make things complicated for him. He is so young, so immature. I'll have to be strong.

"*Accha*[39] listen." I take his face in my hands, the most adorable face. I want to take in every feature, every trace of love in these eyes deep inside me. These eyes emanate so much love. How will I do without looking at them? I inhale deeply and puff out, mustering all the courage to tell him we need to go. But the words won't come out. I struggle to form a goodbye inside my mouth.

But the moment I open my mouth to say goodbye, my eyes betray me and tears start flowing. He cannot bear the sight. He gets restless.

*Oh, so sweet, he can't see me in tears.* He is about to do what he had done to pacify me for the first time he had seen me crying. But he stops and his eyes ask for my permission. I nod. The next moment, I am struggling for some fresh air as his lips meet mine. My heart is ready to jump out of my mouth.

*What did just happen here? I let him smooch me. No! My God, I have messed up big time. I am in danger.*

♥♥♥

**Next day**

I am damn busy today. And it is good for my present messed up state. My racing heart needs work to slow itself down. Amid various classes and editing work, I manage to avoid thoughts of him.

With *Diwali*[40] approaching, a festive atmosphere envelopes the college after lunch. We receive gifts from MD Sir and get a half day off.

After getting our gifts of *Haldiram*[41] packing, we are on the college bus on our way home. The whole bus is littered with *Haldiram*[41] packages of *namkeen*[42] and *rasgullas*[43].

I have reached my stop. I step down from the bus, knowing the danger zone awaits. Walking the familiar path home, he creeps back into my thoughts.

On October 1, 2010, I had resolved to forget him, and by the afternoon he is there looming large in my thoughts. I am growing weak. His every word, the way he took me in his arms, the way he tidied my hair, his lips, everything is crawling back into my consciousness.

*Oh, God, I cannot forget him, I just can't. I know I do not deserve him; I am not a match for him, but why doesn't my heart understand this? Why does it cry? God, I want to give happiness to him, so why do I become so selfish? I've promised him that I'll marry some other person, but God, I can't do this, I can't even think of it.*

After that kiss, we knew our meeting was risky. I promised him I would marry that Chemical Engineer. But interestingly, the Chemical Engineer turned down the proposal. He has a girlfriend, Mother told me.

With all this turmoil going on inside my heart, I reach home. *Bhabhi*[26] has made my favourite *rice and curry*[44], but it tastes insipid. Sitting on the sofa in the so-called drawing room that looks more like a storeroom,

I am just trying to stuff myself. *Bhaiya*$_{4}$ is lying on the sofa cum couch. Suddenly, a shriek comes from upstairs. We run upstairs where Mother is lying on the floor, not even able to move. She had mounted on a ladder doing sweeping for *Diwali*$_{40}$ and fell on the floor while trying to move a little farther.

"Mother, I told you; I'll do it today after coming back from college," I say while supporting her, but she is not able to move.

*Bhaiya*$_{4}$ and I manage to take her to the nearby bed with great difficulty. There appears to be some serious injury as Mother is continuously whimpering.

The day before *Diwali*$_{40}$, when people are decorating their homes, I am at Dr. Anand's Hospital. Mother's hipbone has been fractured.

Today Ruhaan is coming back from Delhi. He has just called me to inform me. I inform him I am at Dr. Anand's, though I don't tell him the reason why.

All the tests are done. I have come downstairs from my mother's room to buy medicines and find the most pleasant surprise of my life. He is sitting on one of the waiting chairs.

"You?" My face, which was dull a moment back, suddenly shines like a hundred-watt bulb.

"Yes, here are the English notes. Now read them and teach me. I need to cover this topic of English to crack IES."

I know he is lying. He has come because he had sensed I was sad. We both go to the canteen of the hospital. Sitting with him, I forget all my problems, along with my pledges of forgetting him. He is my oasis right now in this terrible hospital where I am terribly lonely.

He shoves out a carry bag from his backpack and offers it to me.

"What is it, pillow?"

"Yes, your mother must need this."

I shrug, but keep it anyway.

I get so much emotional that I recite to him the poem that I had written, pouring my conflicted feelings into words,

"This feeling of doubt will always remain,

And it'll also give you pain.

But is this pain more than my love?

Isn't it love that is everything else above?

Can't my love wash all your fret and worry?

The only thing I want is to keep you hale and hearty.

I know you want to take me in your arms,

Even I want to feel your warmth.

But can physical union only make us one?

Don't you feel our souls are already in unison?

A union so strong that none can break,

You know at the very thought (of breaking) my heart aches.

We can't change God's plan whatever will be will be,

But my heart always says that you'll always remain with me.

Because

I've been made to love you only and to bear your baby my feminism,

Only this much I know and nothing else

My life begins with you and with you, it comes to an end."

On hearing the poem, he says one thing and leaves me abashed, elated, and happy.

Taking my hand in his, he says, "You will bear my baby only. That's a promise."

Blood flushes through my cheeks, turning them tomato red.

This *Diwali*[40] is the best *Diwali*[40] of my life. Mother got discharged at our request, as it was *Diwali*[40]. I am the merriest girl on this earth, lighting earthen lamps and candles, head over heels, in love. I look at the rows of lightened houses for hours the way I used to do as a kid. I talk for hours to Ruhaan.

Ruhaan is leaving after *Diwali*[40] and will not turn up for one entire month.

We are not talking much, as he is busy. But we have got close, very close, so close that we don't need to explain to each other anything. Even he has started reading me.

It is said that tough times bring people close and this one month has brought us closer. With Mother and *bhabhi*[26] in bed, as *bhabhi*[26] was eight months pregnant, I became the man of the house. Juggling exam duty, my mother's care and also household work in the biting cold, Ruhaan was my only solace, my pillar of strength.

I had read somewhere that winter is the time to rest, take care, eat, read and get cosy with your loved ones at home. In short, to do all those things that can bring you comfort, warmth, care and Love at home. And I would say that in this period, I've got my home. Ruhaan means home to me. Even his thought brings all those things- comfort, warmth, care and Love- the things one requires during winters.

Good times may connect people, but bad ones bind them forever and that also in such an acquiescence way that no words are needed to explain anything.

# 14

# When Love Reigns

Today marks our reunion after a full month of physical separation, but emotionally, we were growing closer. It's our first official date today; without any restraints. And we've chosen our beloved English Department as the setting.

As we settle on our respective stairs- I on the third from the bottom and he on the one above- he requests that I recite the poem I shared at Dr. Anand's. Blushing, I recite it coyly, observing the emotions play on his face. His nose flares as he takes the piece of paper from my hands, his eyes boring into mine all the while. His Adam's apple hitches, and he takes me in his arms.

My right ear rests on his heart, and I can hear its rhythmic beat, sensing how he is feeling right now. I am amazed by how well my ear rests against his heart when he takes me in his arms. It feels just so perfect. I always feel that his heart beats inside mine, and in this moment, that sentiment feels tangible. Now I know why I felt so restless all these years. It is because my soul yearned for its other half, which she has found now. With him, my soul feels complete, contented, and at peace. We fit so well, like the pieces of a puzzle, understanding, and listening to each other's soul, even without uttering a single word. I know in this very moment that he is my soulmate, the missing half that my soul longed for. Our connection transcends physicality.

Ruhaan takes my hand and leads me to the washroom. Let me tell you, the English Department, in fact, all the departments remain closed on Sundays, so there is not a single soul in here. Today, as we look into the mirror, he checks how we look together. It's endearing.

'What?' I cock my eyebrow.

"Just checking how we look together." He looks so cute when he does these little things.

I lift my eyes to have a look at the picture in front of me. He, in his white t-shirt that accentuates his athletic body, is looking killer. And the moment I look at the girl in the mirror- brown complexion, straight shining black hair, a bulbous nose, small eyes and dark lips – my smile evaporates. Not a single feature is in the right proportion.

I wear a long face.

'What?' his eyes enquire, expressing innocence.

"I'm not a match for you." I release my hand, come outside and sit on my designated stair, but instead of sitting on the one above me, he joins me on mine. He takes my hand in his, tucks my hair behind one ear, places my head on his chest, and pats me lovingly, echoing my father's endearing words,

"You are the most beautiful girl in this whole world, Puchu. "

*Oh My God, these words are so magical.* Leaning against his chest, I can hear his heartbeat, dhak… dhak… dhak…

"That day I told you the Chemical Engineer must be very lucky, but today, I say I'm very lucky." Now, he is stroking my hair and I am feeling so very cosy. My head nestled on his chest; almost buried in it, while he pats me like a baby, stroking my hair. Nothing can be better than this. This is heaven, this is ecstatic. Someone, please shoot a bullet in my head right now, at this very moment.

"Promise me you'll never leave me," he demands as he fiddles with my fingers.

"Promise," I reply, as he locks his fingers inside mine, pecking at them.

"I promise, and you also promise you will never leave me. Even if someday, I shout at you and ask you to go, you won't go, but hold me tightly, promise me."

"Promise," he says, making my head rest against his chest as if I were a small child.

Listening to his heartbeat and getting concerned, I ask, "Hey, are you OK?".

"No, but how do you know?" His voice is muffled.

"You know your heart beats inside mine. I can hear it clearly; beating here," say I, putting my hand on my heart.

"Let me listen." He attempts to put his ear on my heart.

"You dog," I tease, punching him and attempting to escape.

He grips my hand tightly; pins it behind my back and takes me behind the water cooler, which is adjoined to the stairs. He puts his hand across my waist and my phone rings.

"Yeah, Maa[45] coming," I speak into the phone. The rain has started, and drizzles create a romantic ambience.

As I sit behind him on his scooter, completely mum, remembering the moment when his fingers had tickled my waist, the small drops tease me, sending a shiver below my spine.

Mother isn't home. *Bhabhi*[26] is at her mother's house. *Bhaiya*[4] and Mom have gone to her place taking gifts for the baby. *Bhabhi*[26] has given birth to a baby girl. Alone at home, I complete chores and head upstairs with my phone.

The night is beautiful after the evening rain. The wind carrying the fresh scent of damp earth feels like a feast to the nostrils. It is so soothing that it can put a normal person to sleep. But on me, rather than a lullaby, it works as cocaine. Every gust of the cold wind brings back the memory of his touch making my heart jump. It is cold, it is chilling, and still, I don't go inside. Lying under the star-studded sky, I dial his number.

"Hey bro," he answers after three rings.

"Busy?" I enquire, decoding the hidden meaning behind his 'Hey bro'.

"Yes."

"With family?"

"Yeah, with father, collecting payments," he whispers.

Lying on the terrace, I gaze at the stars and play a soothing song on my phone.

The phone rings. No need to be excited, it is Mother.

"Hello, *Maa*[45]."

"How are you? We're not coming today; we will come tomorrow. You ask Pooja to sleep with you, and lock all the doors before going to sleep."

"No need for Pooja," I grumble.

"No, listen, call Pooja, otherwise I'll remain tensed."

"OK, *Maa*[45]." I don't oppose it as it is no use arguing with *Maa*[45], but I will not call Pooja either. I am in no mood to spoil my romantic mood.

I check all the doors, latch the front gate and come back to the terrace. I am gazing at the stars, trying to find out the Great Bear Mother used to show us as kids when the phone buzzes again. This time, it's Ruhaan.

"Hello, Puchu."

His tone suggests he's alone, elevating my spirits.

"So, have you collected the money?" I ask.

"Yeah."

"What happened to you today?"

"What?"

"Nothing," I flush.

"Now come on, tell," he pleads, displaying childlike enthusiasm.

"Why did you take me behind the water cooler?"

"To drink water."

"Yeah, to drink water behind the water cooler," I tease.

"Yeah, to drink water from your lips," he says dreamily.

Tongue-tied, I turn red.

"But your mother played the villain."

"She saved me instead." I blush. "You know you are a real sham; you don't look so *chaalu*[22]. What an innocent face God has given you."

"Thank you," he responds graciously.

"For what?"

"For calling me a *chaalu*[22]."

"OK, listen, once you told me you get physically attracted, is it true?"

"Oh, that……. Yeah, haven't you seen all those pictures with Reena, Tina, Meena?"

"Jokes apart."

"Yeah, I do, I confess."

"So, you get attracted to any girl?" I feel like crying.

"Yes, I get attracted to boys even," he answers in an affected, serious tone.

"*Yaar*$_{36}$, you are impossible. OK, leave it."

"Do you think so?" Now he is serious. "You know; you are the only enchantress who has entranced me."

"But you live in Delhi. You must know so many beautiful girls; modern girls."

"*Na Baba Na*$_{46}$, God save me from these Delhi girls. Now they are what you call *chaalu*$_{22}$."

"But don't you think I am not a match for you?"

"Hey, come on, you don't know what you are to me. You are a walking, breathing poetry, Rhythima. You add music to my otherwise tuneless life. You are my soul's symphony that plays on the strings of my untuned heart, providing it peace and solace."

"Someone has become a poet."

"That's the charm of your love."

"But you are fair and I am so dark."

"Who says you are dark? Have you seen your neck?"

"What?" I zap.

"That is your real colour, you know how much I crave to… coming Mom," he speaks out of the phone. "*Yaar*$_{36}$, Mom is calling for dinner. I will talk to you later."

"OK," I say, feeling like a fish out of water.

"Good night!"

Alone again, I'm left in the middle of something. Yet, a new thought emerges- his parents. He says his father is very strict. *Will he ever give his consent for our marriage? What am I doing, just flowing with him or pushing him to flow with me? I should not make things too difficult for both of us.*

# 15

# The Birthday

Another month has passed without us meeting, and I'm eagerly expecting something special from him.

It's my birthday tomorrow!

It's not that my birthday is anything special. But I hope it holds a special place in his heart.

I am in my lab, adjusting the computers for the next lecture as joy surges within me. His call lights up my phone. I do a *jhiingalala hur*[47] in my mind, expecting he has called to fix a date for tomorrow. He never calls me during college hours. But what he says breaks my heart to bits and pieces.

"I'm leaving today by the 9 o'clock train; it's urgent."

*No, this can't be happening. I've waited patiently for this day for one entire month, and now he's telling me he is leaving today. A prank, perhaps? But no, the seriousness in his tone stings.*

I feel a lump in my throat as I cannot pronounce a single syllable. I am so upset that I get restless. Students have thronged in the lab and tears are swimming in my eyes. However hard may I try; I cannot blink them away. I stand up and decide to take a half-day leave. Within minutes, on the pretext that my mother is unwell, I get leave. Tears did the deed.

Now at the University Third Gate, uncertainty clouds my thoughts. I try his phone, but he doesn't pick up. This angers me even more. I don't want to go home, so I take an auto and head for the city. I decide to go shopping to calm my agitated spirit. I am trying a dress on when he calls, enquiring about my location. For the first time in my life, I am so mad at him, I yell,

"What does it matter where I am? You go to your IIT."

He pesters again and again to fish my whereabouts out of me. I give up giving him the address. Within minutes, he reaches me. I am out of my wits, completely, thoroughly. Standing in the middle of the city of Kurukshetra, I lash out,

"Why are you here? Who has called you?"

I am burning with anger. And, he, wearing a solemn expression, responds, "I've just come to give some of my mom's clothes for dry-clean."

He has not come to meet me! This revelation adds fuel to the fire, intensifying my anger. My words turn sarcastic. "Then do your work. Why waste your precious time? I'm going to *didi's*[48] house."

After walking a few steps, I call him again. I know he has come to meet me. Even in my blind rage, I can read this man.

"I'm going and never in life try to talk to me again. Goodbye," I speak into the phone.

"W… wait… Where are you? Please tell me; I'm searching for you. Please tell me?"

"I'm heading towards Aggarsain *Chowk*[5]."

"Please stay there, please, I'm coming."

I want to hastily escape from this place; from this insensible man, but stay put. He comes. I shout again. He pleads, "Please sit."

I sit on his scooter, lips pouted, eyes red, breath heavy.

He takes me to our Lovers' Point, the English Department. But it is not a Sunday. So, there is no chance of us going inside to sit on the enclosed stairs of the English Department. In the open, he pleads, "Please forgive me."

I am on fire. "Please, for what? You find a girl of your match for yourself."

His heart sinks. I can see it in his eyes. I feel a gust of guilt course through me. *Why am I putting him through this?* But my anger has gotten over me. Gathering himself, he again pleads, "Just give me one chance. I'll take great care of you. I'll always be at your disposal."

This melts me.

*Is he a conjurer who always manages to trap me,* I wonder! He is not romantic in the least. Still, I can't help but love him. He is a *Bhondu Ram*[49] who doesn't know that girls need to be pampered. I mean, he hasn't even brought a small birthday present for me. Just a flower from him would have been a cherished and priceless gift for me. I feel like singing, *main kaa karu Raam mujhe Bhondu mil gaya*$_{50}$.

But I have chosen my *Bhondu*$_{49}$ and I love him with the whole of my heart.

♥♥♥

**22/12/2010**

I am so thrilled. My dear *Bhondu*$_{49}$ is going to make up for all the past grievances. We are going to Karan Lake in Karnal to make up for my birthday.

He arrives to pick me up from Pipli *Chowk*$_{5}$. Despite the biting cold, the sun provides a comforting warmth. I am wearing a black woollen *kurta*$_{54}$ with some silver embroidery on it, paired with silver leggings. I had bought that *kurta*$_{54}$ on my birthday when he had shattered my heart. *Bhondu*$_{49}$, dressed in a mustard shirt complementing his fair complexion, surprises me by opting for a bike instead of his usual scooter. My overprotective darling has brought a windcheater and helmet for me.

He makes me wear his oversized white windcheater and helmet. I look like I'm preparing for a journey into space. He puts my bag inside his backpack.

I comply with all his instructions, only rejecting one- to sit cross-legged. Looking at my dress, I am not ready to do it. But he won't budge and I have to obey. It's for my safety, he says.

Can a person be charmingly annoying? Ruhaan certainly has mastered this art. As if all this helmet, windcheater and sitting cross-legged wasn't enough, he asks me to hug him tightly, again for my safety. Again, I have to agree. In the mirror of the bike, I can see a broad grin etched across his face. His eyes are smiling the very same smile I can die for that starts somewhere behind his throat and reaches his eyes, making them shine. Every once in a while, he touches my hands softly and rubs them to make sure I am all right.

*Oh God, this guy is so cute!*

After searching for a long we can find a place which we suppose is secluded. But there is no seclusion on Karan Lake. Two boys pass on a bike, passing comment,

"Hold her tightly lest she may run."

We laugh our heads off. Soon we fall silent. But this silence is not disturbing. It is happening to us these days. Sometimes we don't talk, just sit in each other's arms, and it feels like we have talked a lot, and have bared our souls to each other. It's not only me who is an expert in reading Ruhaan, even he reads me a lot. When we don't speak, our souls seem to commune. With him around, I don't feel incomplete anymore. It feels like a part of me was missing all these years, which made me restless. But with him, everything is perfect, just perfect. He radiates love and care even without saying a word.

We have been sitting like this for some time, revelling in each other's company, when he suddenly jumps up, making me stand. We reach Sauvé Greens. He starts taking my photographs. I am not camera conscious any more. Even I have begun to enjoy these photo sessions. Photographs make memories, he says, and he wants to keep a memory of every single moment spent with me, and so do I. He is so jealous when I pause, putting my arm around Ronald at McDonald's, that he doesn't even click the photo. He sulks like a kid.

# 16

# Every Day Is Valentine's Day

It has been more than one month since we last met. As Valentine's Day approaches, I can't help but dream of meeting him, despite knowing he is busy. He hasn't met me since 22nd December. Being the diehard romantic I am, I have made a card for him in the shape of a heart where I have drawn him in one corner and have filled the rest of the heart with 'Puchu loves Sham, Puchu loves Sham.' The card has come out so great, at least it looks so to me. And I am dying to give it to him. Not only time and colours have gone into making the card, but also plenty of bravery. I had to hide it behind the curtains every time I heard any footsteps. It took the whole of my day as I had to hide it at least 9-10 times with watercolours dripping, fearing it would get spoiled, and finally, it has got spoiled!

My *Bhondu*[49], engrossed in his studies, seems to have no time for me. I hoped he would make up for his past mistakes by doing something special on Valentine's Day. But he is he and will always remain the same boring, studious, busy bee.

He is busy. He has to submit his project report on 14$^{th}$ Feb. Can you imagine, on 14$^{th}$ Feb? He has no time for lovey-dovey. I am mad at him.

There is a kind of irritation that has been gnawing at my heart. The fault is not mine. He's just too cute to live without.

It's evening. I have concealed my anger till now. But now it's too much. It needs to be ventilated or I would burst out. So, here he is calling. And I am all ready with my ravings.

"I tried to forget you," I shout into my Nokia phone.

No answer. *Hasn't he done enough to enrage me that now he is playing 'The Silent Woman?'*

"Why don't you understand? I am getting irritated because you don't talk to me. It feels like I'm a burden for you."

His defence is a simple, "No!"

*Just this? Not even a single romantic word on Valentine's Day.*

"Yes, it's true, that's why you can never make time for me," I persist in articulating my complaints. "You come to your home every weekend but can't make time for me, neither for my birthday nor for Valentine's Day. I don't understand where in the world you remain busy. You must have a girlfriend in Delhi. Why one? You must have so many. I know you just pity me. You thought, oh, the poor girl loves me. What would become of her without me? So, you, out of pity, accepted my love. You don't love me. You haven't even said it today, on Valentine's Day. It all proves that you are just pitying on a lovelorn girl. I don't need your pity. I'm fine alone." I smack the side of the bed as I end up whimpering.

Still getting no reply, not a single word, I hang. I know I've given him pain by saying all those things. Now his sad, tired face is swarming in front of my eyes. But I am not going to call to say sorry. Though all I want to say is:

*Hey, jaan*$_{51}$ *you and only you are mine in this world. I behave badly and cause you heartache, but I never mean it. You are the only one I believe to be mine, on whom I feel I have all the rights. That's why I become so possessive that I even shout at you. Please never take me wrong. My heart is filled only with love for you.*

But no, I will not call.

Congratulations! Valentine's Day is over with not a single loving word from my *Bhondu*$_{49,}$ let alone some romantic date. Aargh!

♥♥♥

The next day, I carry my sullen mood to college, questioning whether he loves me or just pities me.

In the evening, while heading home, my phone rings. He asks a simple question that instantly lifts my spirits,

"Would you like to have a cup of coffee with me?"

He had asked me the same thing almost two years back. But today it's altogether different. This one sentence has all the power to bring my smile back. I am full of energy and zeal again. My heart is throbbing, ready to dance.

He picks me up, and we find ourselves in a public place, at café New Way near the English Department of KUK. Taking my hand in his, he apologises to me. When he does this, he looks so cute and honest that I feel guilty for having told him all those things. I find his nose more vocal than his mouth. It conveys to me things he never says. His moods, I can judge from his nose. He is crinkling his nose now and then, which means he is very tired. To meet me, he finished his project in one night, which he was supposed to finish in three days. Proof that he has burned midnight oil is visible under his eyes; half-moons are formed there. There are lines around his eyes and they look exhausted. Still, they are emanating love for me. These two eyes can emanate so much love. I feel such a pang of guilt in my heart that I recite my poem to him,

"I know I make you cry

Don't know why

But my heart only knows

How much I want you to smile

And smile and smile

I know I make you tense

Don't know whence

But my heart only knows

My love for you is so deep and immense."

He gets very emotional; like a small kid who has got his mother's love after a long time. He tells me about his family members, about his *dadaji*[52], whom he loves very much and who is no more. He shares intriguing tales from his time working as a spy. He says he misses him. He doesn't have a sister, just one younger brother. Listening to his stories, I didn't notice when I ate from his plate. He is thrilled to notice it, but when I appear conscious about finding out that I am eating from his plate, he gets a little sad. After finishing the *dosa*[13], he gets one Coca-Cola. As I am listening to his stories, he suddenly gets serious and, taking a draught from Coca-Cola, asks, "You won't drink from it, will you?"

I don't know what comes over me. Snatching the bottle from his hand, I put my lips to where he had just put his. I check him out from the corner of my eye. There is a smile on his face; more precious to me than my sanctity. Strange, but I ask him a question, "You feel quite alien in your family?"

He nods, which gives me more nerve to ask,

"Do.... you have some issue with your father?"

"My family is different. It's not like a regular family." Now the smile has disappeared. His eyes look empty and his face is clouded. I cannot make out what is going on inside his heart.

"Don't worry. Now I've come, I'll solve all your issues, I'll bring you closer." I try to relieve the pain visible on his face. But I don't find that smile that starts somewhere behind his throat and reaches his eyes. He looks rather disturbed.

"I want to go very far away from my family. I pray to God to give me a job somewhere very far away."

*So Rhythima the Great, you were right; there is some problem.* I don't know what, but whatever it is, I just want to resolve it and also his pain.

"Hey, I went through your notes, so when do you want to start?" I try to change the topic.

"Let's start now."

"OK, very well, but we can't study here, so let's go somewhere else," I suggest, and he at once comes to the solution, the English Department.

So, we step up the stairs of the English Department one more time, but this time to study.

As we sit at our fixed Places-I on the third last stair and he on the one above me, I open the book to discuss what should we start. As I tell him about the first rule on Common Errors in English, I find him looking at my arms. I am wearing a sleeveless *kurta*[54]. He is not a good student in the least. I ask him to repeat the rule. He repeats,

"Anything... everything in this world is a noun."

"For example?"

"This book, I, you, we, your hands," says he, taking my hands in his. "Your arms."

I nudge him in the stomach. "Look, I am quite serious. You told me you are weak in English, that's why you could not crack the exam last time. Now I don't want this again, concentrate," I chide him.

"I'm thirsty," he whimpers.

"So, w.... hat, here is the water cooler drink water and come?"

*I am trying to teach. And here he is more interested in water-cooler.*

"Do you want to study or not?" I am angry now.

"Yes, but um... err... I was wondering you must also drink water; you must be thirsty." He grins.

"OK, fine." I get up with a jerk to drink water. He follows.

He catches hold of my hand; takes me behind the water cooler and the next moment he puts his arms around my waist saying, "Happy Valentine's Day." His touch just sends a chill down my spine, making me want to melt in his arms. But I say, "Wait a minute," and bring the card- I had made for him- from my bag. Looking at the card, he once again tries to take me in his arms when we hear some footsteps. It is Mr. Joseph, a professo in the Language Department that is in the same building.

I hasten to the stairs. Mr Joseph, taking me to be a student of the English Department, stops me to inform me about the uses of the Language Course for Literature Students. He hasn't changed. He used to do the same when I was a student here. I reply, "Yes, sir, I'll join," and climb down the stairs. Ruhaan follows me after a while. He comes to the lawn where I am sitting. He gets very emotional after seeing the card. As I sit on the lawn cross-legged, he comes and lies down, resting his head in my lap. I stroke his hair. He closes his eyes and seems to be in a slumber. After a while, he breaks the silence.

"Would you love me the same way as you do today, even after five years?" His voice is a whisper.

"No," I say, adding, "I'll love you more with each passing day, with each passing minute."

"Over the years you will see faults in me as happens in every relationship and then you won't love me the way you do today."

"I promise, my love for you will never fade with time. It'll only deepen."

"Really?".

"Yes!" He gives me a side hug while still lying.

"You know what, I talk to God. It… it might sound weird to you, but I do."

"I trust you." He is not in a disposition to talk but to feel.

"And that day when we decided to carry on with our relationship, I asked God if I should do it. You know what did He reply?"

"What?"

"The guy you are moving with is my child, a sweet innocent child, and has his flaws. So, once you hold his hand, never leave him. Hence, I have promised to God that I'll always love you with all your flaws, but the fact is I can't see any flaws in you."

He kisses my hand and keeps lying in my lap as if he is taking a rest after a long time. There is serenity all around.

"But will you love me the same way, even after five years? I'm a bad girl, a selfish one that you'll soon come to know."

"You are the sweetest, nicest and most beautiful girl in this world," declares he, this time kissing my arm.

"Hey, what are you doing?" I feel a titillation in my body.

"Your arms are so pretty."

"I know you have had your eyes on my arms since morning, and what about studies *Aashiq Sahib*[53]?"

"How can any student focus on studying when the teacher is so sexy and comes wearing a sleeveless *kurta*[54] to teach?" He smirks and I feel my face turn red.

"Hey, I'm thirsty. Come on, let's drink water."

"You'll have to wait to quench your thirst," I retort, moving my fingers in his hair.

"You know what is the best feeling in this world for me?" he asks in a groggy voice.

"What?"

"When you move your fingers in my hair," he smiles his real smile while saying this.

I keep moving my fingers in his hair, declaring, "If it is so, I'll always do this."

Today, I have learned that love is not bound to any particular day. When two souls are in unison, they need not be physically together on some special occasion. In fact, for them, every day is Valentine's Day.

# 17

# And the Studies Begin

I am determined to teach him. He has told me he'd never be able to remain happy in life if he couldn't make it to crack IES. And his happiness, his smile, is my weakness and strength; I can do anything to keep that smile intact. With this goal in mind, I devise innovative teaching methods, incorporating stories and poems into the lessons.

Today, I am going to give him the first vocabulary lesson. He has grown very naughty, always thirsty. So, along with the story method that I have devised, I think of one more strategy to spice up the lessons. I promise to give him one peck after completing each lesson in either vocabulary or grammar.

Eager to teach him, I start the lesson with a rhythmic tale,

"The boy was amiable, cordial, sociable, friendly, and cream

Always falling into reverie at the sight of his dreams."

I explain the synonyms of 'amiable'– 'cordial', 'sociable', and 'friendly.' Now it's his turn to recall the synonyms.

"Lovable," he whispers, taking my fingers in his hand.

"No, not lovable." I smack his shoulder.

"Ouch." He rubs his shoulder, pretending I hurt him. "Am I not lovable?" He holds my gaze. I pretend to be angry.

"Sham, this is study time."

"But I'm thirsty."

"OK, first complete today's lesson, then we'll look after your thirst."

"Please, one…. Then I'll be serious," he insists.

"You know you failed last time because of English. Now I don't want you to repeat it. Complete the lesson of vocabulary then, I promise."

Pulling a long face, he agrees.

Continuing the story, I speak, "And what he used to see was the zenith, the apogee, the pinnacle, the summit, the peak."

His attention is keen, and he recites the synonyms. Elated, I continue the story.

"But capricious and whimsical as he was, he'll soon abase himself, which will cause abeyance.

And the girl will again try to abase the feeling of abasement

Trying to appraise him of life's rich pageant."

He tries hard to understand. After telling him the meanings of all the words, I try to teach him grammar. But, closing the book, he says,

"Hey, you promised."

"What?" *How much do I enjoy pulling his leg?*

He holds my hand and takes me behind the water cooler.

Resisting the advances, I protest, "This is not right. I'm telling you, I'll..."

But he closes my lips with his hands.

Taking me in his arms, he says, "You are the most beautiful girl in this world. I will always be there for you by your side. Let me complete my M. Tech and I'll talk to my parents."

There is so much honesty in his words, I believe every single one of them. He flares his nose as he always does when he is naughty.

"Will you do me a favour today?" he nearly begs. "Give me a kiss." He seems to be fighting some battle.

I hug him, saying, "I love you, and I will wait for you till the end."

His heart is thumping like a clock on the wall saying, dhak.... dhak and such a tumult is going over there that for once I think of fulfilling his wish but then just blush at the idea.

I always wonder how I can read every emotion going inside his heart. Most of the time it feels to me it's beating not inside him but me.

# 18

## DECISIONS AND DILEMMAS

Even a week without him feels like an eternity, and he will not turn up for two whole months. And this time he has not left me me, but he. *Ranjha Ranjha kardi ve main aape Ranjha hoi... mainu Heer naa aakho koi*[55], is the ring tone of my phone these days. Each day passes imagining about him, and each night dreaming about him. *Jaise filmon mein hota hai, exactly waisa hi is happening to me, zubi doobi zoobi doobi*[56]. Yes, I am also busy preparing for my UGC exam. But, I miss him.

The months have passed, and it is the fateful day.

He is going to sit for the IES Exam today.

He calls me in the morning and I wish him luck. Soon after, he tells me he is going into the exam hall; I sit down to pray. I pray to God, no, not to do some miracle or tell him all the answers, but to give him strength to complete the whole paper. I keep on saying *Om Namah Shivay*[57] for two hours, and then his call comes.

"How was the paper?" I ask eagerly.

"OK."

"Only, OK?"

"It was superb," he says, leaving me more than glad, allowing my racing heart to relax a bit.

"Now go eat something and prepare for tomorrow, and yes, take no tension and study a little today, just take an overview, just relax, and watch some movie."

"Okay, okay, I'll do as directed. Now relax."

I am keeping my fingers crossed.

The next day, the ritual repeats. The exam, the prayers, and the call- each moment laden with anticipation. He sounds happy.

Finally, it's time for the last and crucial exam.

He seems low. I send him an inspirational message to heighten his morale and sit down to pray. But after two hours, I am not able to concentrate. I am restless and finally get up. I am biting my nails, waiting for his call. Strange, the three hours are over, yet he hasn't called. I wait for another half an hour before dialling his number. The line is busy. Another half an hour passes. He calls.

"How was the paper?" I ask. My heart is suffocating in my ribcage.

"Fine!" His voice carries a hint of sadness.

"Just fine?"

"Not even fine, to tell the truth. I don't know what happened in the last hour. I was blank. I wrote nothing. I won't be able to make it."

"Don't worry, you have done your *karma*[58]. Now don't worry about the fruit." Trying to change his mood, I add, "You want to quench your thirst?"

No reply comes. He says he would have to hang as his mother is calling.

With the IES Exam over, two long years of waiting also conclude.

He's now a postgraduate with a promising job which marks the beginning of a new chapter for us. We can look forward to locking horns. The prospect of meeting his family looms large, accompanied by nagging fears. *Will they accept me? What does it mean when he says that his family is different?* I am trying to shoo these fears away while covering the fifteen-minute distance from my home to the bus stop in the morning when he surprises me with a call,

"Hello *Ji*[73], *pink dupatte me kya haseen lag rahi ho*[59]," he teases me playfully, imitating some hooligan.

"What?"

"Aren't you wearing a pink *dupatta*[60]?"

"Yes, I am, but how do you know?"

"You once said I'm a conjurer, so I know."

"Where are you?" He comes from behind on a Ranger cycle in a black Bermuda and white t-shirt. His legs are way fairer than his face.

"So, you have started following me, you rogue," I taunt him.

"*Kithe challe sonyo gobi daa phool banke*[61]?"

"Oh, ho, someone has learned to talk after going to IIT," I tease.

"Come, sit on my cycle. I'll drop you."

"No, thanks!"

"Are you all right?"

"Yes."

"Any problem?"

"No."

"Now, are you going to tell me?"

"I'm fine; my bus might come any time, you go."

"No, I'm not going. You are coming with me."

"I can't, I've got to go."

"Take leave today."

"Not possible."

"That I don't know, but you are coming with me." He has never been so adamant earlier.

I call the HOD to inform I am on leave.

Sitting across from each other in Hotel Saffron, he takes my hand in his. The dark ambience of the restaurant with slow music playing in the background adds to my gloomy mood. He asks me why am I worried and I tell him the reason. Would his parents like me as I am older? He suggests not to reveal my real age, but I turn down his suggestion, saying it is not fair. I don't want to build our relationship on a lie. I panic. He tries to pacify me that age isn't a big deal and soon our talk turns to the question of belling the cat.

"Have you talked to them?" I ask.

"Not yet. I've just returned."

"Yeah, I understand," I say, getting even more worried.

"Look, you trust me, don't you?" His nose is crinkling now.

"Yes, more than myself."

"Then give me time."

"My family is searching for a match for me. That was my luck that the Chemical Engineer said no himself as he was having an affair, but this time I won't be able to say no."

"Why?" His nose crinkles even more.

"I told you about my cousin, Vijay *bhaiya*[4], who has always been with us through all thick and thin after Papa's demise; he is telling a match and I can't say no to him."

"You don't worry, I'll talk to Papa," he seems perplexed as he tries to assure me.

"You need to hurry. You are not getting it; I cannot say no to him. The boy is a doctor and is doing practice under bhaiya[4]. He knows him very well; I just can't say no."

"The boy is a doctor?" he asks, making his already big eyes bigger.

"Yes."

"Then you must say yes."

"What are you saying? You are from IIT having the best job in your hand, and is money everything?" I am shocked.

"I will not take that job."

"Why?"

"I told you earlier I want to become an IES Officer. This time I won't be able to make it. I know very well. So, I must prepare for it again, and in that MNC, I know I won't be getting any time."

"Oh."

"But I want your permission first. Do you want me to do that job? If yes, I'll join."

"Hey, I want to see you happy, that's it. If you are not happy, I cannot remain happy, though I'd seen dreams of going to Pune." I mock a pout, crossing my arms across my chest.

"But there is one more thing we have to decide before leaving the job."

"What?"

"My parents would never allow you to continue your job, so if you want to do a job, I will take the job in Pune."

"Hey, I want to be with you and want to see you happy always. I want to live with parents having their blessings."

"Are you sure about it? You must first give a thought to it and then decide," he reiterates.

"I'm quite sure I want to live with your parents."

"Then don't worry, just trust me."

"But you will have to hurry; I've to reply to *bhaiya*[4]."

# 19

# How to Bell the Cat

A day, a week, a month, two months slip away, and the status remains the same; he hasn't spoken to his parents.

"I've got to answer *bhaiya*[4], why don't you understand?" I exclaim into the phone.

*Bhaiya*[4], a father figure to me, has asked my opinion, and I have got to answer him.

"I'm.... I'm," he stammers.

In the evening as I cover the familiar fifteen-minute distance from the bus stop to home, I sense his presence trailing me on his scooter. Irritated, I feign ignorance, pretending not to notice him. Driving parallel to me, he pleads that I sit behind him. Eventually, relenting to his persistent pleas, I reluctantly join him, and we head towards Hotel Parakeet.

"The first boy saw me here only; I must have said yes then," my anger spills as we settle on the red chairs. I avoid looking at him.

"You are right, you must have said yes. I'm not a match for you." There's pain in his voice. My anger melts.

"You would do nothing," tears well in my eyes as I speak.

"I've talked to Father," his voice falters as he speaks. "Yesterday after dinner, I announced, I've had a girlfriend for the last two years."

"And?" I press.

"Father got furious, and I said, I was… I was just joking." He passes a limp hand through his hair as his nose crinkles.

"You can't tell your parents that you love a girl. Strange." I am all worked up. "Tomorrow I'm going to *didi's*[48] house. They are also telling a match and want to show him to me. The boy is very rich having property of crores and you want only that for me, so I'll say yes."

His heart sinks and I leave. His nose is crinkling more than ever, but I leave.

Jaya *bhabhi*[26] calls me, telling me about the boy Vijay *bhaiya*[4] has chosen for me. *Bhaiya*[4] is equal to God for me. I would have said yes if Ruhaan had not come into my life. But I can't cheat *bhaiya*[4] who I know loves me a lot and always wants my good. He is a father figure to me. I have no choice but to tell the truth,

"*Bhabhi*[26] th… th… there is a boy who loves me," I get meek as I speak. Nobody in my family can suspect me of having an affair. But, to my amazement, *bhabhi*[26] doesn't react. My mother already had some idea-mothers are mothers after all-and must have hinted *bhabhi*[26].

"Do you love him too?" *bhabhi*$_{26}$ asks.

"Yeah!" I can say only this much and add, "*Bhabhi*$_{26}$, please don't tell anybody."

After talking to *bhabhi*$_{26}$, one thing that is killing me is what *bhaiya*$_{4}$ would think of me.

♥♥♥

These are holidays, and I am going to Chandigarh per plan- to stay with *didi*$_{48}$ for some days. When I am at the bus stop, his call comes but I don't pick it up.

He is calling again and again.

Almost at the hundredth call, I pick up. I shout into the phone, "I'm going to *didi*$_{48}$ for some days to see a boy she has found for me, you… you just go…….," and I hang up. I know he is crying, his face immersed in a water pool and his nose running. But I recollect what *bhabhi*$_{26}$ had told me, 'Be tough, don't get emotional.' I check myself from calling him.

It's 3 in the afternoon. I have reached Chandigarh. I'd thought I'd get busy there with *didi's*$_{48}$ kids and won't think about him. But strange, for the first time in my life, I am not enjoying playing with kids. I am trying hard but cannot bug myself up. Something is pricking. His tear-smeared face is dancing in front of me. Again, I resist the temptation to call him.

By evening, I am unable to resist. So, I call. "Hello, sir," I say through the phone. The very word 'sir,'from me makes his heart sink, I know. "Here's good news for you. As you always wished, I've got a very rich boy as a match. I don't know if I'd ever be able to love him, but he's rich and that's what's more important, isn't it?" I taunt.

"Stop, *yaar*[36], stop, you know even the thought of seeing you with somebody else kills me."

*At least I have managed to snatch some reaction out of him.*

"Then why don't you talk to your parents?" I am not angry anymore, but grumpy.

"I'll, I will, Puchu… but give me some time. When the right time comes, I'll tell them. I promise," he is almost begging and I hate it. I want to be a queen of my king, not make him a pauper. I need to fix it right now.

"Can you come to Chandigarh?"

"Yes, I am leaving right now."

On the pretext I am going to meet my friend, Meeta, I go to meet him. I try to remain tough, but my heart betrays me. I trust him more than anybody else. I know he'd never dumb me.

We meet at DLF Mall. Those two days of torture by me have left him all drained of energy. He hasn't shaved, his eyes are puffed, and he also looks weak.

"Are you all right?" I ask as we settle on our respective seats in the theatre to watch the movie *Teri Meri Kahani*[62], a movie with no *kahani*[63] at all.

He doesn't reply, but I know he is crying. He thinks he can befool me in the dark, but I know him like the back of my hand; even better. Now I can't be tough with him anymore. I lean into his seat. I can feel his breath on my right ear. I turn my face towards him; I can hear a sniff. I place my lips on his left cheek and give him a wet kiss. He hugs me. We leave the theatre as we are not interested in the movie.

After searching for half an hour, we find a fine place, a park-like patch of land. You see, there is no dearth of fine places in the city beautiful. He lies with his head in my lap and I start moving fingers in his hair. He closes his eyes as if taking rest after a long time. Seeing his innocent face, I know for sure that this boy can never ditch me. I trust him. To relieve the pain which I have given him, I move my lips to his ears and whisper,

"I'm sorry."

"Trust me," says he, taking my hand in his. "I'll marry you. Just give me some time."

"I trust you," saying this, I hug him.

We remain like this for a long time. There is no need to explain anything as our hearts beat in synchronization.

♥♥♥

The weather is so delightful. There are clouds spreading flush, orange hues in the sky. I love the monsoon and it seems it is about to come. As I leave home, there are signs it will rain, but I head for auto. My heart leaps. He gave me a call to give some good news.

"What's the news?" I asked when he called me in the morning.

"I'll tell after meeting you," he replied.

I practically know what it is, but I want to listen to the complete story.

As I take an auto, it starts drizzling, and he calls.

"It has started raining. Don't come."

"But I'm already in the auto," I say fearing he would call off the plan, but he is worried about me.

"You come to Pipli; I'll be waiting for you there."

"OK."

As I reach Pipli, he is already waiting on his scooter for me and together we head towards our Lovers' Point. Small raindrops are falling on me which feels great along with him. My hand on his shoulder and he holding my hand whenever he has to put a break, it's just perfect. How caring he is! The more I get to know him, the more my heart rises in love with this guy.

As we have reached the English Department and settled at our respective places, I ask impatiently,

"So?"

"First, let me see you," he says, gazing at me. "You are looking killer in this red suit," says he, still looking at me. I realize my chiffon suit has got a little damp. But right now, I am growing impatient to hear the good news, and he hands me a letter. "Appointment letter?" I shrug.

"Yes! I've got the job at PMIT."

"Oh, congratulations." I am elated, though I never knew he was searching for a job. It can happen only in love. You revel in the happiness of your beloved, forgetting about your worries.

In the meantime, my phone rings. It is Jaya *bhabhi*[26]. "Has he talked to his parents?" *bhabhi*[26] asks. "No, not yet," I respond. She asks me to do it fast otherwise she would have to tell *bhaiya*[4]. I only reply with a yes or no.

After talking to *bhabhi*[26], my mood suddenly changes.

"So, you want a treat?" he asks.

And I explode, "Treat? Treat for what? For my marriage with some other guy."

"Look! It has started raining," he tries to change my mood. He knows I love rain.

Pretending as if in a great hurry, I come downstairs and begin walking, but in the wrong direction. Sensing my mood, he comes following and asks, "Where are you going?"

"To hell!" I am boiling.

"Hey come let's talk. What has happened?" he again tries.

"Nothing, let me go," I say, turning my face from him.

He grasps my hand and takes me to a nearby place; I have got all wet. He gives me his handkerchief. But I smack his hand.

"By the way, you are looking ravishing," he attempts again. It enrages me more.

"You want this, only this. All boys are the same. *Bhabhi*[26] is right, they want just one thing but can't commit. Now you have had enough of your enjoyment, just go." I cry.

"What has happened?" he asks tiding my hair.

"Nothing, just go." I smack his hand again. "I'll marry that Dr and you will be more than happy. You want only this, don't you?" saying this, I leave. He follows me for a while but then stops. It has started raining heavily. I walk a few steps but have to stop. It has started pouring cats and dogs.

I have reached NIT. I go under a shed and cry my heart out. But suddenly it starts to lightning, and I get reminded he is standing in the rain and he is the eldest sibling. Getting scared as it is said lightning falls on the eldest of siblings, I run to him. He is standing in the same spot, numb, undone, and devastated. I approach him.

"Come on, why are you standing here? It's lightning." I drag him to the nearest department.

"I love you," he utters as if in a stupor.

"I know; I know that, but why don't you talk to your parents?"

"I will. Earlier I was not in a position as I did not have a job. Now I can talk to them as now I'm independent."

*Oh, stupid Rhythima! Didn't you have that much sense in your head? He has found a job so that he can talk to his parents.* Now the thing gets into my head.

He is still sad, so I hug him, but he doesn't touch me. I put his hands around my waist, but he resists. He is stone cold.

"You think my love is only physical? I want only one thing?" He is hurt.

"I'm sorry. You know, I was angry. That's why I said all this, and in fact, my love is physical," I say, caressing his wet face. Nevertheless, he doesn't touch me.

So now it's time to use my *Brahmastra*$_{64}$.

I take his face in my palms; tilt his head; bring my lips closer to his and mark the first stamp of love from my side.

How can my *Brahmastra*$_{64}$ fail?

In a jiffy, he lifts me in his arms. I am around one foot above the ground, in his arms. The next moment he makes me lie on a table nearby. In an instant, his one hand is on my waist and another on my wet lips. There is a strong tickling in my body as the chilly wind sends a chill through my wet clothes. But then we hear some footsteps. He goes to check. Meanwhile, so many thoughts float through my mind.

*The heart is such a complicated organ; I feel it creates most of the problems in the world. Sometimes I feel like intersecting mine to find out how it behaves in so diverse ways. Sometimes it behaves like a kid, chuckling at the trivial things as mine was doing for the last two years; other times like a spoiled, adamant brat getting mad at the slightest of things as mine was a moment back; and sometimes like a romantic singing love songs as mine was behaving at the moment, ready to break all the barriers. But thank God! It also has an elder sibling called Reason who has come to my rescue right now.* I get up tiding my clothes and come out of that perilous place that provides tables on its veranda for lovers to do naughty stuff.

He soon comes to me with the expression, 'What happened?' written on his face

"Let's go, it has stopped raining," I reply, and we head home.

Today I have decided I would never shout at him again and would give him his time.

As I lie early on the bed on the pretence, I have got tired, my heart sings songs, getting romantic as it is raining again. *Rimjhim rimjhim, runjhun, runjhun, bhigi bhigi rut mein tum hum hum tum, chalte hain*[65], it sings. I want to talk to him and do some nonsense talk which we haven't done since he has returned from IIT, but I think better of it and let sleep take over me.

I read his message, first thing in the morning, 'Everything set, talked to father.' The thing I have been waiting for a long makes me feel cold. I am terrified thinking about the reaction of his parents. I cannot wait and call him. His voice is groggy when he says, "They have agreed," and hangs. How much I love this groggy voice of his! The thought that now I would get up listening to his groggy voice and seeing his face first thing in the morning makes me blush.

I take a deep sigh of relief and tell *bhabhi*[26], but she is still doubtful. Later in the evening, *bhaiya's*[4] call comes, and he takes his number from me.

# 20

## The Cat Is Belled

Ruhaan has got a job in a semi-government college, a job which his father always wanted him to do. His parents have agreed, and everything seems set, but it is not so. My family still is not sure as they haven't had any word with Ruhaan's parents.

It's his birthday! I have bought a showpiece- a heart of a crystal with a couple inside it- for him. I have also woven a sweater of off-white colour for him. During winter, I noticed that he wears hand-woven sweaters under his shirt, the same as my mother weaves. So, I learned from Mother and weaved one. I am excited; just too excited to give it to him, which has taken me four entire months to weave. *Would I be able to weave love and find a nook in his parents' hearts the same way I have woven this sweater for him? Oh, why do I always start biting my nails at the thought of his parents? Why do I freak out? Relax Rhythima!*

Anticipation hangs in the air as I wait at the red corner table in Hotel Parakeet. I am trying to make out the patterns drawn on the yellow wall when I spot him opening the glass door of the restaurant. Why does my heart always leap on seeing him? But he doesn't look happy. His face is rather pale, and stubble has overgrown his chin, which is quite unusual for him. Generally, he is clean-shaven. He says he shaves three times before coming to meet me so that his stubble doesn't prickle my smooth skin. And when he rubs his newly shaven skin against mine, I drool over it. I have even grown to love his aftershave. *But what's wrong today?*

As he reaches me and takes a chair across from me, I sing, "Happy Birthday to you, Happy Birthday to you," and give him the gift, which he doesn't even bother to give a cursory look. I enquire about his birthday plans. They don't celebrate birthdays, is his curt reply. "Even we don't at our home," I say to make it sound casual. On my insistence, he opens the gift and feigns to be happy. When I ask how he likes the sweater, his answer is, "Nice, but I can't keep it?" *How can he be so callous?* I try to persuade him to hide the sweater at home if he can't show it to his parents, but he doesn't understand how anything can be hidden at home. He can keep it in his cupboard. I smack the table with enthusiasm as I suggest. But he isn't impressed by my ideas. He has broken my heart, but I say nothing. He already looks too disturbed.

"What has happened? Any problem in college?" I ask. He says he is just tired. "You must be happy. It's your birthday and your parents have also agreed," I probe even more. I need to know why is he so sad. I can't bear it; this sullen look on his face, I just can't.

I am also excited to listen to the whole incident and how he told his parents. How did he cajole them? I am beaming, but he is very low, and this makes my spirits low too. Are this man's moods contagious? Sensing a drop in my spirits, he tries to pull himself and responds,

"I went for a walk with father, we took a complete round of Sector 5 and I told him."

"Is he mad that's why you are so sad?" I ask.

"No, we must leave." He gets up.

"You promised me you would tell me everything. Now I make you swear on me, tell me." I grab his hand, pulling him to take a seat.

"I told him, I'll leave home if you………"

*My Gosh, he is sobbing!*

"How could I say such a thing to my father? Why didn't my breathing stop before saying this to him?" and he breaks down. A usual feeling of guilt and being the real culprit cascades upon me. I have always been the culprit, the guilty, the bad daughter, the bad sister. *How do I get out of this? How, God?* Sensing my mood, he changes the topic,

"Yeah…. your Vijay *bhaiya*[4] called me to take father's number."

Now it's my turn to be low. My heart has got sunk. I'm choking again. Tears have already pooled in my eyes.

♥♥♥

How boring our dates have grown since this marriage thing has crept into our relationship. We are only crying, fighting and blaming each other while earlier only one thing concerned us, i.e., each other's happiness. It is so even now. We are indeed fighting and crying, but these fights always bring us closer.

I return home with a heavy heart and the feeling of that of a culprit who is making a nice boy do wicked things. All I feel is remorse right now. I cannot find rest after making him burst into tears. So, I sit down to pray,

'God, you gave me whatever I asked for, a pure soul with a pure heart filled just with love, not any trace of hatred. But God, I've realized that I don't deserve him. He is a pure soul, an angel, so an angel must get a fairy. His life partner should be like him, pure-hearted and thoroughly clean. And it is not I. I am not a fairy. I made him do this. God, I can wait for him my entire life, can pass my life without him, but can't cause him heartache. If for marrying me, he must go through all this, I don't want to marry him. God, I want you to do one thing, give him the best life with the best life partner, one of his parents' choice. In my madness, I had forgotten that I was not a match for him.'

My heart is crying. But it's not just my heart that's crying. I always have this strong feeling that his heart beats inside mine, so how can he not know when my heart is crying? This happens to us all the time. When one of us is sad, the other knows it. How? It's a mystery. Maybe it's true that our hearts are not two but one. Tears are rolling down my cheeks when he calls.

"Are you all right?" he asks.

"Yeah!" I can't utter more.

"You are crying?"

"No."

"I'm sorry. I made you cry. I'm sorry. Things were not that bad as I behaved they were."

"I am sorry. I know you are a wonderful son and you said all this to your father just for me. I'm a bad girl, a terrible one, I already told you. But you know what my problem is, I can't see you in pain. I know this thing will disturb you always. I can't undo what we have done, but we can do one thing. You tell your parents it was a joke, and marry a girl of their choice."

"Are you mad or what?"

"I'll go from your life."

"And what would become of me?"

"Your parents will find an excellent match for you; they are so nice."

"It's not like that. You know what, my father wants me to marry a girl who is not even well educated and a complete dumbo and way too young."

"Why?" I snap. "I know there is nothing like this. You are making up stories just to prove I am right for you."

"Only you are right for me, Rhythima, just you. No one else can complete me. You are the music of my life."

"But I can't see you sad. I can't bear the sight."

"I'm not sad. I'm more than happy. I'm on cloud nine. You don't have the slightest idea what would become of me without you."

"Really?"

"We are tailor-made."

"And your father, he must be hurt." Even the thought of hurting the father of such a pure soul hurts me. If Ruhaan is so great, how great a soul his father might be, I always wonder.

"No, you don't know him."

"Soon I will, and bring you two very close. Watch for it. And yes, you are my oasis in the desert, Ruhaan; you are my entire *Jahaan*[66]."

"I know. Yeah, I forgot to tell you, your Vijay *bhaiya*[4] called Papa. They are coming to our home."

"When?"

"You don't know?"

"No!"

"They wanted to come tomorrow, but Mother had to clean the house, so she wanted four days."

"Four days to clean the house?"

# 21

# Preparing to Be the Daughter-in-Law

'Four days to discuss the matter with family' (the reason I told my family) - the news spread like fire in the jungle in my family. Those who are now aware of my affair are firing questions to which I have no answers.

"Four days to discuss with family?" my sister asks.

"Four days to discuss with family?" *Bhabhi*[26] raises her eyebrows.

"I'm telling you they are not interested at all, just giving you sweet pills," *didi*[48] tells Mother. Mother has got so worried that I am going to go through hell for the remaining four days.

The D-Day has arrived. Vijay *bhaiya*[4], my brother and my mother have left for Ruhaan's house.

I am keeping my fingers crossed.

Risha George, my best friend, has come for a week from Dubai where she stays after marriage. So, I have called upon her.

"Hey Rhyths, you have transformed!" Risha shrieks in pleasure as she hugs me.

"Really, what's the change?"

"Come on, girl, I have never seen this spark in your eyes earlier. It speaks volumes about your transformation. And where has all that inferiority complex gone?"

"Magic of love," I chuckle. My drooped spirits uplift for a minute after having a drizzle of praise on them and I get into the auto-pilot mode. "You know, Risha, I want to stand on the highest peak and shout to the world that I am in love. Love is an incredibly beautiful force that brings out the best in you. I mean, why do people fight? Why do terrorists do horrible things? Help them find their soulmates, and there would be no war, only love and peace."

"Wait… wait… wait… give me a break. What has gotten into you? You never emanated so much positivity before. Where had you kept that Rhythima hidden all those years?"

"Love, my dear, love has made me a better person. Every moment I spend loving him, I rise more in love."

"Rise?" Risha cocks her eyebrow. "Fall, I think, is the right word. You fall in love, right?"

"That, dear Risha, is the difference." I hold both her shoulders and make her twirl with me. "I never fell for him, but have risen in love with him."

"So, all set," she hits the nail while sitting on her queen-size bed.

"No, nothing is set." I pout, dropping my face while taking a seat beside her. On her prodding, I tell her everything sharing even my qualms and seek advice from her, which she readily gives me.

"It is a love marriage, so never expect that you will be welcomed there. In an arranged marriage, the girl is of the parents' choice, so they have to accept her as she is, even though she is worse than the one chosen by their boy." We both giggle while doing a high five. "But in a love marriage the girl is not of parents' choice, so it would be hard for them to accept the girl even though she respects them and cares for them a lot," she says.

"OK, that thing I'll keep in mind, but I have one more fear, cooking. I'm not very good at it and they want specially this from me." I bite my nails.

"Hey Rhythima, you already know cooking. Why are you so worried?"

"Um… how do I tell you? In our families, the *bahu*[67] must be *sarvgun samppan*[68], not like yours, that she will be accepted as she is. We need to change upside down inside out. They want perfection."

"Hey relax, you will learn with time. But never lie to them. Don't pretend to be a master chef when you are not. Just be honest, that way things will take time, but they will settle."

"Yes!" I sit straight, inhaling deeply, trying to grasp every word of what she is saying when her mother enters with tea. On knowing I am leaving my job, she gets suspicious.

"Why do you want to leave your job?"

"Aunty, it's prohibited..."

"Mom, she has no interest in money," Risha interrupts before I can say anything, as Aunty doesn't know it is a love marriage.

I wonder how love marriages are frowned upon in the sacred land of Krishna and Rama. While we bow before Gods celebrated for their love, how can we despise people who dare to love? The moment you mention you are in love, you are alienated. You get your character anatomized by self-acclaimed connoisseurs.

I get those two talismans injected in my mind, 'Don't expect you will be welcomed there, never lie about anything,' and head home.

Life can never be free of surprises, and when it's a delightful surprise, life seems so beautiful. When I am expecting the worst, I get the best news. Both the families have talked to each other. And guess what, they have agreed.

*Ah... such a relief.* Everything went well.

*Bhaiya*[4] puts a gentle hand on my head asking, "Happy?" It feels like my father is standing in front of me asking me this question. I heave a sigh of relief that *bhaiya*[4] doesn't despise me after coming to know about Ruhaan and me and loves me the same way. It feels as if a great burden is off my chest and I can breathe again.

So, everything is set. Both the families have talked to each other. I am so happy. Though I can't declare it officially as Ruhaan's parents want time, at least one year so that their son gets settled first, still I am happy. The best part for me is I won't be on display any more. So, no need to be worried.

I am thrilled and have started seeing dreams, dreams of a life with Ruhaan. Ruhaan is also happy, but some fears keep disturbing me. *Will I be able to please Ruhaan's parents while he is so alienated from his father?*

♥♥♥

Now I am busy teaching Ruhaan and learning to cook as I have to make a good daughter-in-law and Ruhaan an IES officer.

I am teaching Ruhaan on weekends. Today he is in no mood to study so I voice my fears to him,

"Sham, I'm afraid."

"Afraid of what?"

"Your parents.... will they like me?"

"What fear now? Everything is settled."

"But how'll I please them? My friend Risha George said they would not welcome me into their family, as it is a love marriage?"

"Yeah, she is right, but by and by, they will accept you."

"But w... hat if... if they dislike my cooking, and I am not beautiful also?"

"You are beautiful, and exquisite, and don't worry about cooking. My mother will teach you."

"Really?"

"Yes! You know, my mother is a very nice lady. She is a goddess and will love you like her own daughter."

"But I'm not the right match for you. You will find a thousand of girls far more suitable than me."

"But I want only you, and I'm also afraid."

. "Why are you afraid?"

"Won't your family see any flaws in me?"

"My mother already goes bananas over you, *jiju*[3] and *bhaiya*[4] also like you."

"Really?"

"Yes, but your parents have not even seen me."

"They want to."

"What?" I am shaken up at the thought.

"Should I call them today?"

"No, no please, I'm not ready. Look how I am looking," I beg. My heart is hammering even at the prospect.

"OK, OK, relax, don't worry. We'll do it some other day when you are comfortable."

He hasn't touched me today and is sitting at least a mile away from me. *Why is he behaving so weirdly today?* I wonder. Suddenly he gets up, saying someone has come to meet him.

I can see him coming towards me with a middle-aged couple. Now it hits me. No! They are his parents. I have no idea where to go. I want to run; hide; be invisible, whatever is possible.

They are standing in front of me. I fidget a little and then dive at their feet. They don't put their hands on my head to bless me. Ruhaan seems the happiest person doing much of the talking. All I want to do is spank him for putting me in this tight spot, not without even informing me. But he is smiling his real smile that starts somewhere behind his throat and reaches his eyes, making them shine. *Oh God, what won't I give to keep this smile always alive on this most adorable face?*

We four, one couple and one couple-to-be, are sitting on the lawn of the English Department. His mother looks for everything to his father's approval, who has an air of domination and patriarchy around him. I am sitting with my eyes bent and calling Ruhaan names in my hearts of hearts, as I am not in a presentable condition at all; even my hair is tousled.

Ruhaan's father says, "We won't allow you to continue your job. Leave it right now and learn all household chores, and no laughing or chit-chat in my house. I won't tolerate anything like this. And one more thing, no one must know about your relationship. We'll just show it as an arranged marriage. You better take care of it."

Unprepared and dishevelled, I grapple with the demands imposed by his father, while his mother just seems a shadow of her husband with no individuality or opinion. Yearning to be Ruhaan's better half, I nod to everything without even paying heed to what they are asking of me.

# 22

# The Thing Most Dreaded and Desired

Naina is on her way home when she calls me. Her playful voice echoes through the phone as she jests, "What happened to you? Why the sulking? Found another Mittal at IITM?"

Getting no answer from me, she demands, "Where are you right now?"

"Going home," I reply in a low voice. I am overwhelmed by a sense of despair following the encounter with Ruhaan's parents.

"But where are you?" she enquires.

"In the auto," the sinking feeling persists as I respond.

"Where have you reached?"

"Somewhere near Panorama."

"Get off the auto."

"What?"

"I said, just get off the auto, wait for me in Panorama."

"W… what, have you gone mad, Naina? Do you know what time it is? You'll get late."

"Just wait for me in the Panorama."

"But… N…"

Before I can articulate one more word, the line goes off. So, I step out of the auto and go inside the Panorama & Science Centre to sit on the lush lawn. Nostalgia hits as this place hides so many beautiful memories of my 'on-the-job training' with my college gang. I try to uplift my spirits. Otherwise, Naina would know. I amble over to the nearby water cooler to wash my face. I am splashing the chilled water on my face when I hear Uncle Scrooge,

"You are mean." A tiny figure of Naina that looks thinner is standing, arms crossed over the chest and chin upwards.

"Hey, it's not that," I defend wiping my face with my green *dupatta*[60]. "I am busy."

"One is never too busy for things one wants to do. You always make time for him," she retorts, almost accusingly.

*Is she spying on me?*

"Whom?" I feign innocence.

"Now stop that drama. I know the bug has bitten you."

"And how did you come to know?" I can't resist a smile on my face as I see her sulking.

"It's all over your face."

"Oh… I admire your face-reading prowess. But, madam, you have just seen me after a long time." I can't help grinning.

"Then it's all inside you, I… I know that's it. Ask no more questions, just tell me the complete story. I would have been happier, though, if you had approached me yourself." She twitches her lips; arms still crossed over her chest and turns away from me.

I embrace her slight frame from the back, wondering how small she is. "OK, sorry. Listen, I want to tell you everything. Let's sit." I sit on the bench nearby.

"Who's holding you?" She cocks her right eyebrow while joining me.

"But tell me, won't you be late? It's already five-thirty, your mother…"

"You don't worry about her, just tell me." She is all excited.

"How is it even possible, Naina," I begin in a dreamy voice, "a stranger enters your life and becomes an indispensable part of it. So important that you can't imagine your life without him. You start enjoying every tiny bit about him; the way he smiles; the way he looks at you; the way his nose acts according to his moods; the way he touches you; the way he tidies your hair; everything, even his aftershave."

"Kiss?"

"What?"

"Has kiss happened?"

"Naina!" I blush as I speak. "It's not about that. I mean, it's not about being physical." I move my hands in the air, trying to convince her.

Undeterred, she teases, "Oh, ho, my *Sati Savitri*[69]. Then what is this, the way he touches; the way he takes you in his arms, Hun?" she imitates me.

Flustered, I stammer, "I… I …didn't say the way he takes you in his arms."

"So, hasn't he? Is he a dumbo like you?"

"He has. And he is not a dumbo," I admit, while I blush. Naina always tricks me into spilling the beans.

Naina, wrapping her arm around my shoulders, says, "There is nothing wrong with being physical. It's normal, okay? By the way, are you normal? I mean, the way you used to shriek at the name of Mittal. And now all this kissing wissing."

"I am quite normal, okay? And your Mittal is a pervert. Yes, I do like when he touches me."

"Uh… uh… where do you like it the most?" Naina, in her playful banter, plods further.

"Waist…" I blurt out, realizing Naina's trap soon after the word is out of my mouth.

"Nainaa… you always do this to me."

"What have I done, darling? I haven't even touched you. And aren't you going to kill me?"

"Naina."

"See, this is the magic of love. You don't get angry anymore. Enjoy it, Rhythima. You are lucky to be loved by the person you love. You know it's God's greatest blessing to be loved by the person you love. Nothing can be more beautiful than this. Just let love happen; don't run away from it. Look at me," she trails off.

To celebrate her friend's newfound love even as her own heart shatters into a myriad of pieces embodies the true essence of friendship for me right now. In this bittersweet moment, only Naina can exemplify such purity of soul–revelling in my joy while nursing her own broken and aching heart.

"Hey, Naina." I embrace her little frame in my arms, wishing to be able to do something for her; for her troubled heart. But Naina is no damsel in distress, she is our warrior princess.

"You know, I always wanted to make you my *bhabhi*[26]," she sniffs as she speaks in her Uncle Scrooge's voice.

"Your *bhabhi*[26], *Na Baba Na*[46]."

"So, what's the story?"

I narrate the entire story, beginning from our first meeting to the current predicament, voicing my fears.

"But there is one problem."

"Go on."

"I'm not sure whether they like me. No one has ever liked me; not even my family. Then why would they like me?"

"See, if you didn't get the love you deserved from your family, it's not your fault. Yeah, sometimes, our family members- unintentionally though - make us feel that it's our fault and we start believing that we aren't good enough, whereas it has never been our fault. And we have every right to heal ourselves by accepting the love that God is sending us. So, just Let Love Happen. You don't need to do anything else."

"They don't want me to continue with the job," I speak in a choked voice.

"So?"

"I mean… Huh… I've agreed, but… you know that's an important part of my life."

"Look Rhyths, if you ask for my opinion, I don't know all this important-shimportant. I know one thing. After joining IITM, you have faced the thing you dread the most, along with getting the thing you desire the most. And it's the same thing. Now, you decide whether you want to keep dreading and run away from it or accept it as God's blessing."

Perplexed, I question, "What are you saying, Naina? I am not getting you. What thing are you talking about?"

"That only you have to crack. I will just suggest not everyone who loves you will leave you. So don't let the love of your life go; just let it happen. And see, I have taught you to express. Thank God you accepted your feelings for… what's his name, *yaar*[36]?"

"Sham…. no… Ruhaan, I call him Sham."

"Yeah… thank God you accepted your feelings for your Sham… I am happy for you… now I have got to go."

"But tell me… what's the thing that I dread the most and desire the most both at the same time?"

"Think… you will know."

With this she bids goodbye, leaving me to unravel the mystery.

# 23

# When Nightmares Come True

What a great relief it is when, after seeing a long bad dream, you realize it was just a dream, not reality. What a deep sigh of relief you take when you open your eyes and say, "Thank God it was just a dream." I have been having the same experience for the last 4-5 days. Every night, a sense of restlessness and fear encroaches upon me when I find myself caught with him. Two months ago, I had a dream where a professor at my college saw me with him and I was afraid he would spill the beans. I must have cautioned, but the yearning in my heart to meet him was much stronger than the feeling of ennui that I experienced in my dream. So, I went to meet him the next day. I was frightened and wanted to cancel the plan, but my desire to see him; that keenness to be with him; being seen by him; getting ready for him; and being in his arms overpowered the fear of being seen by someone.

Last night also I had that dream. I was crying for him, my heart heavy. Surrounded by a wall, there was no way I could reach him.

The dream has left me grumpy.

This morning, I opt for an auto ride instead of my routine walk, still shaken by the dream's echoes. Waiting at my stop, I decide to call him when the bus arrives.

I sink into a seat beside Anu Ma'am, a faculty in the IT Department. Bubbly and being from the same department, she always reminds me of Naina. But the normally jubilant Anu Ma'am looks pale today.

On an impulse, I enquire, "Everything all right?"

Anu Ma'am first hesitates but eventually confides, "There was a death in my neighbourhood this morning." She wipes away a tear, her voice quivering. "This girl, Naina, was my friend. Such a bubbly girl. I am not able to come out of the shock."

Naina. My heart sinks. I do a quick calculation. Anu Ma'am is from Shahbad, Naina's city. *No... Rhythima,* I mentally chide myself, *is there just one Naina in Shahbad? Stop racking your brains. Just don't even dare think of it, she can't be....*

"Yes, Naina Chadhha. She is; I mean, was my neighbour."

"Naina Chadhha..." My heart sinks even deeper.

"Yes, she had recently shifted to Chandigarh to work with Telecom. She too was in IT. I met her just a week back. I still can't believe it. And she had had typhoid... how can......" Anu Ma'am's voice tapers off.

*No... God... no, you can't do this. This can't be true... my Naina. I know that's not true. It's just some other nightmare.*

"Ma'am." Anu Ma'am shakes my shoulder.

"Y.... yes." It feels as if some ghost has touched me.

"Her mother...Naina's mother..." I mumble.

"Poor lady...was not even in her senses. How she adored her."

"No...she did not...she never did...she was her stepmother." I am almost in a slumber.

Anu Ma'am is stunned to hear this. Soon she gathers her senses and asks, "Did you know her?"

"She was my second family." Tears start rolling down my cheeks. I have never choked so badly in my life. The world has suddenly ceased to be. My vision is blurred with tears. I feel a familiar ache; helplessness; frustration; annoyance so many emotions all at the same time. I have a feeling of déjà vu. I have gone through this earlier also; the same feelings of ache, helplessness, frustration, and annoyance. A strong urge to yell, to shout, to shriek, to howl infuses me. I want to get down on my knees and howl like some madman right now.

Naina's complaints that I don't speak to her anymore come haunting me. She was right. I had gotten so busy in my life that I had stopped thinking about her.

But suddenly this. The thought; the reality that I can't get to see her anymore; can't talk to her anymore, makes me feel helpless. It feels like my heart will break into a thousand pieces. The same familiar emotions come visiting. I am hurt; more than hurt, I am infuriated with God for putting me through this once again. *Why me, always?*

The feeling of losing a loved one cannot be described in words. And if there are any words to best describe it, you feel your heart has been ripped off the ribcage and stamped over by a pair of shoes having a thousand nails in them.

*I can't take it; I just can't bear it.*

Anu Ma'am helps me in taking leave by apprising the Director Sir of my condition. The authorities take care of leaving me home.

I don't know how it all came into action, but I am home right now. It's 10:45 am. I am lying in my bed. There's this continuous nuisance caused by some *ghazal*[70] hammering in my head. After many failed attempts to get away with this disturbing noise, I get up to find it's my phone ringing.

It's Ruhaan. *How?* My heart cries. *How does he know I need him?* He never calls me during college hours unless it's an emergency.

"Ruhaaaan…" I burst into tears.

"Hey, what happened?"

"Ruhaan, Naina…" I sob.

I can't bring myself up to form those words. Something about even forming those words in my mouth seems wrong, very wrong. I don't want to say those words as if not saying them would change the reality. But this is reality; the damn stark reality which can't be changed. Death is the only reality that no daunting spirit, no indomitable will, can change. However hard you may try to run away from it; it will stand there on tip-toes staring you in your eyes; daring you not to accept it. But how dare you? You can't play a stoic when you are at your worst vulnerable self. When your heart is crushed; trodden with a thousand nails; your every belief in God, the Supreme is shaken to the bits.

"What…what happened Rhythima…what happened to Naina?"

"Ruhaan." I am howling now and scaring the hell out of Ruhaan.

"Rhythima, get some grip…I'm scared. Tell me what happened."

"Ruhaan, Naina… Naina is no more." *No, my heart will break into a thousand pieces and I am in no condition to gather them. God can't do this to me. I don't believe this; I can't believe this.*

"What?" It's Ruhaan's turn to disbelieve now.

"Yes!" I am howling, crushing the pillow against my heart.

"Oh no," he mumbles. "Listen Rhythima, I can't talk to you right now. I have a class. But you try to calm yourself, OK? Where are you?"

"Home."

"Good." He takes a sigh of relief.

"Get yourself some sleep, OK?

"I can't sleep. I am having nightmares, Ruhaan. Promise me… promise me you'll never leave me; promise whatever may befall, you'll never leave me; you'll always remain with me."

"I promise; I promise *jaan*[51]. I'll always be there for you. And let me tell you one thing, Naina has had enough struggles in life. She is in a better place now, trust me. Now you get some sleep. We will talk in the evening."

I am in a toilet, but the toilet has no boundaries. It's an open toilet. Suddenly I find a crowd of people staring at me, laughing. I am shouting for Ruhaan. But he is nowhere to be seen.

I am sitting in a wedding *mandap*[71], getting married.

Now I am sitting on the bed waiting for my groom. I get up with a jerk. The groom is not Ruhaan.

I awaken with a sudden start. I am soaked in sweat, my pulse racing. It was yet another dream; the weirdest, worst kind of dream.

I look at the watch. It's 5:30 pm. There is still half an hour left till Mom's return from the office. I pick up my phone from the bedside and dial Ruhaan's number. He does not pick up.

Even after trying for the umpteenth time, the result is the same- Ruhaan does not answer.

# 24

# When Dreams Come True

It's been ten days since I met him or even talked to him. He knows I am going through a tough phase. Then why is he doing this to me? *Are my nightmares going to come true? Am I going to get married to some other guy? Are my family members right when they say that Ruhaan's father is intentionally delaying matters, never intending to accept me?* I am already 27, they say, way past marriageable age, while Ruhaan is just 24. He has all the time in the world. I feel like throwing up.

Amid this mental chaos, a notification on my phone interrupts my thoughts – a message from Ruhaan. On seeing his name flashing on the screen, my first impulse is to throw my phone away. 'Where have you reached?' he enquires. 'Hell,' I type but then delete retyping, 'Aggarsain *Chowk*[5].' 'Get off the bus in front of Hotel Heritage,' immediately his message pops.

So finally, we are meeting.

Seating at a corner table, I anxiously await his arrival. He doesn't take long to come. Ruhaan appears, wearing an expression of weariness and sadness, as if burdened by lots of errands. Concern replaces my anger, and I find myself asking, "May I ask what happened?"

He hesitantly opens his mouth to say something, then closes it. I place his hand on my head.

"Now I make you swear on me. Tell me what happened?"

"Um... err... huh," he clears his throat and I prod. He begins again, "You remember when Dad insisted that no one should know about us?"

"Yes, I do," I respond, recalling the eerie meeting with his parents. "And you know what? I am having these strange dreams that people have caught us. I'm getting married to someone else."

"Y... your dream came true."

"What?"

"Remember our last trip to Liberty Showroom, when you wanted those sports shoes? We spotted Suhana Ma'am, an ex-faculty in IITM?"

"Yes."

"Her boyfriend Ashok Lathore works in my college and...."

"And?"

"The whole college was talking about my girlfriend the day when Naina...." he hesitates, then begins again, "That day I had called to inform you about that only... you know, to caution you."

"And?" A sinking feeling wraps around me.

"Father came to know."

"And?"

"He…. um, just leave it. I have some other problems at hand right now."

"Tell me… what did your father say? Now I make you swear on me."

"Hey… stop this? Stop making me swear on you."

"I have already done it. And I want every single bit."

"Please don't make me do this."

"At least tell me the nitty-gritty."

"He… he called you derogatory names and told me to forget about you," he confesses.

Tears spring in my eyes as I say, "I knew it."

Emotions overwhelm me, a sense of loss looming large. Everything, everyone I love, and who loves me back slips from my hands like sand. *Why does this happen to me always?* I am suddenly this ball of nerves that will break at a mere touch. But there is one touch that can make me whole, complete. Ruhaan stands up and comes to sit beside me. He cradles me in his arms. I know he is afraid as there are full chances of us being spotted by some known person in the small city of Kurukshetra. I know he is quite afraid of his father, but still he dares. This makes me crave for him even more.

"Ruhaan," I whisper.

"Yes," he replies, his mouth inching closer to mine.

"Will you do me a favour and end it all now?" I impulsively plead.

"Stop it, you silly girl… I haven't even touched you properly yet," he teases, attempting to uplift my spirits. I try to compose myself.

"OK… now listen, don't worry about me. I am not going anywhere. Who is going to put up with me? Right now, I need to sort out some bigger problems. And I need your help."

My eyes lit up at the prospect of being useful.

"I would never be happy if I cannot crack IES," he confesses.

"You will, this time," I reassure him.

"Not possible with the job. There's so much clerical work. I get no time to study."

"So, leave the damn job."

"It's not that easy," he admits, torn between filial obligations and personal aspiration.

"Don't think so much, just do what you want to do; leave the job," I urge, emphasizing the need for him to prioritize his dreams.

"That is what I need to do. This is my last attempt," he discloses.

"But you are not even 25," I remark, surprised by the gravity of his decision.

"Last attempt means it won't be possible after marriage," he clarifies, his gaze penetrating mine.

"So why are you delaying it? Just leave the job?" I press.

"But Father won't allow it, and how will I marry you if I'm not having any job?" he voices his concerns.

"Don't worry about marriage; it can wait," I suggest.

"No, *yaar*[36], you can wait, but what about your family?" he counters, expressing genuine worry.

"I'll manage," I try to assure him.

"And what about the proposals you are getting?"

"Are you afraid?" I get happy as I see fear- fear of losing me- in his eyes.

"Yes, I am very much afraid," he says, taking my hand in his.

"Don't worry about me. I'll die but not marry anybody else."

"Shut up and swear on me that you won't do anything like this," he implores, placing my hand on his head.

Snatching my hand, I say, "No, I can't swear on you. I promise I won't do anything like this, but I won't marry anyone else either. I can't even imagine." Even the thought scares me.

"That will never happen; I promise you I will marry you," he assures me, our connection deepening.

"So, tomorrow give your resignation," I direct, convinced that pursuing one's dreams requires bold decisions.

"But… Father?" he hesitates, recognizing the challenges ahead.

"Hey, he's your father; he'll understand," I encourage.

"No, he won't, I know him, he is… he is a nar…."

"How can you decide without trying, at least try once," I urge.

"When I was in IITM, I applied for one month's leave to prepare for GATE, but he didn't let me. He humiliated me so much that I had to take the leave application back. And……" he is about to say something but holds.

"Then you are lacking in communication skills. You must have the guts to persuade him, at least try once."

"OK, as you say," he says, but he is quite sure of a no.

♥♥♥

Something strange and unexpected happened. It took five days, but Sham's father finally agreed, and Sham quit his job. When his students, who like him very much, asked him why he was leaving, he made an excuse that he was opening his own Coaching Centre. So, his Coaching Centre has also begun fulfilling one of his dreams. He is now a Managing Director. Though the setup is tiny, he is a Managing Director. The sparkle in his eyes speaks volumes. It feels like now I live to see his dreams being fulfilled. How my heart grows when I see that glitter in his eyes. I always knew he has got this spark which he says no one else has seen earlier. He says no one bothers about him; he is no more than an errand boy. But for me, he is my hero, my prince charming, and a legend I will make him.

Now I know our connection was undeniable. All this while, the whole universe was conspiring to bring us together. That's why Sulochana took me for that interview and I got selected, too. The universe has its strange ways of making things happen, which we cannot figure out. But now I know one thing–everything happens for a reason. We might not be able to make out the reason right away, but one day it'll make sense. Even putting us under challenging circumstances is God's way of making things happen for us only. So instead of complaining about things not going our way, we should try to look at the bigger picture, always having faith in God. Always believing that He'll never do us wrong. No matter what He is always on our side.

I feel a sense of purpose in witnessing his dreams unfold. He credits me as his lucky charm, but in reality, it's his unwavering determination and resilience that makes him shine.

As we face the unknown future together, I realize the real charm of life lies in the unknown. None of us knows what lies ahead in store for us, and there lies the beauty of our existence. This unknown gives us the strength to hope and dream. And it is our dreams that make our life worth living. The dreams Ruhaan's eyes see are mine now. What if mine have been snatched from my eyes? I'll make his dreams mine.

The very thought of dreams reminds me of the meeting with Ruhaan's dominating father. He has taken all my dreams from my eyes in the snap of a finger. *Will I ever be able to please a guy who is not satisfied with his son?* Fears come crawling back shaking my faith a little.

# 25

# The Problem

**8/07/2012**

He has reappeared for the IES Exam, and also the one-long year his father had asked for is over. I have told no one about my meeting with his parents. Talks about tying my nuptial knot with my Sham are going on. And I find myself caught in a whirlwind of confusion.

The real challenge begins as the meeting is finally scheduled for Monday. Ruhaan's father suggests, "Every family has its problems. Let's meet and talk."

Hell breaks loose at the mention of the word 'problem.'

"They are just trying to postpone; we have been waiting for a year and still they are saying there is a problem. I'm sure they will say no," says my mother. I know that it's just her concern that's making her say all these things, but still, I feel like I am a burden. Suddenly I have this strange feeling of breaking every tie with Ruhaan. I don't like the idea of forcing myself upon them. After all, that's what I am doing. Ruhaan's family is dead against this match. *Why am I forcing myself upon them? Why?* I am devastated.

There is almost an entire week left for that meeting and my concerned family has just made the mountain out of a molehill.

In college, while making calls during admission days, I receive a message from Meera *di*[48], my eldest sister. Even before I can vocalise a hello into the phone, she begins,

"They are still saying there is a problem; I don't think they will say yes. I am dead sure they will put it off."

I break down. Even I am at sea wondering what to do. *What would become of me?* I hang up on the pretext I am on duty. I try hard to manage. After a lot of effort, I can concentrate on my work when I get a second call from my second sister, Radhika *di*[48].

"What is going on? What do you want, girl? Just tell us what we should tell people. If you want to remain a spinster for your entire life, tell us. You go your own way, but have mercy on us. Let us live. You have made a drama out of your life, but at least don't make one of ours."

I cannot answer; I am so filled with tears. Moreover, I am in college; I cannot create a scene here. When it becomes intolerable, I go into the washroom and make a call to Ruhaan,

"So, your parents still have a problem, OK fine *yaar*[36], if they don't…."

"If you are upset right now, don't talk to me," Ruhaan interrupts. "Why do you people always make a big deal out of a small matter and distort the facts? I was there and my father used the word 'problem' in answer to your brother's question. That's it."

Even Ruhaan is yelling at me. OK, my family does it all the time but Ruhaan? I cannot take it anymore and hang up saying I have to perform my duty.

After a while, I get restless. I can't bear his sad face, which is reeling in front of my eyes all the time, so I call him again.

"Are you sad?" I ask, despite myself.

"No, I am not," he lies.

"I know you are. I made you," I insist.

"You know you can't make me sad," he sounds a little better.

"Why did you shout at me?".

"I don't know, *yaar*[36]. My problem is I get perplexed very easily."

"Um.... I'm having a waiting, bye." It's Radhika *di*[48].

"Yes, *didi*[48]?" I speak into the phone.

"To whom were you talking?"

"Um...."

"Listen, now stop making calls to that boy. He is a sham and listen, he will not marry you. He is just making a fool out of you. Ask him what that problem is. He must know."

"He doesn't know," I mumble.

"What sort of person he is. For three years he has been fooling around with you, making false promises and now there is a problem and he does not even know what it is. If he does not know what is the problem, why is he talking to you? You give me his number; I'll talk to him."

I have no energy left to retort, so I give his number to *didi*[48].

At lunch, deciding to avoid becoming a topic of ridicule at college, I sit alone in my lab. I am in no mood to eat anything. I am done with being yelled at. Ruhaan calls.

"So, my sister talked to you?" I am ready for some more tug of war.

"Yes, *yaar*[36], but I don't know if she is so nice or was just pretending. She talked nicely."

"So now you have started finding faults in my sister as well. She is not a pretender. She cares for me."

"I am just saying she is nice. Why are you shouting?"

"You know what I've been going through. My sister said just forget him and we'll find some other match for you. Can you imagine what is it like for me?" I almost shriek.

"Hey Puchu, don't cry. How did you think I would marry somebody else? What would become of me? You don't worry; you will become only my wife."

"I'm sorry I spoiled your mood."

For the first time, even a talk with him could not relax my mind. So many doubts have been injected into my heart that it is aching. It feels like I would cease to be.

# 26

# What's the Problem

It appears that God has decided to heap challenges upon challenges in my life. The more I try to solve the problems, the harder they punch me in the face.

Finally, the 'problem' is out of the bag, creating even more problems.

"Now we know what the problem is. He doesn't have a job. Wow!" Radhika *di's*$_{48}$ sarcasm cuts through the air.

"He has a Coaching Centre, and he is not saying no," I weakly defend.

"This is the limit! Do you still trust him? I must salute you for this. He says he is not having a job. This is the problem, and you still believe he'll marry you? You have faith in him and not in us. Tell me one thing, will you eat money? Can't he manage two ends of meat? He is completely under his parents' thumb, a *dabbu*$_{72}$. They won't say no, but they will delay everything and torment us until we back out. He is very clever; giving you sweet pills. Mark my words; he will not marry you. He is young, with all the time in the world, but you... you are growing old. Your age of marriage has already passed. It's not that I am saying all this because I enjoy it; I am saying all this because I care for you. I am not fond of spending money on phone calls. I am doing this because I care for you. He is not your own; we are," she says all in one breath.

If it were just for me, I could wait for my Sham for my entire life, not just for some years. But when my family pushes, I get pushed. My sister's words keep echoing in my head, and doubt creeps in for a moment. *Have I been made a fool?*

For the first time in my life- though transitory- a thought enters my mind.

*Have I chosen the wrong boy for me?*

I call Sham and say the worst things I can say. I repeat my sister's entire talk, pointing out his dad's clever strategy to make us back out.

"I am not blaming your dad. He loves you a lot, and he wants to save you. He wants to save you from marrying an older girl. But why did he promise us a year back? As a father, he is doing well, but he has no right to play with others' lives. I don't worry about myself, I'll live alone, but what would become of my family? I am giving them pain. I have no right to put them through this. But why am I telling all this to you? You love your parents, so you must abide by them. You enjoy," I yell.

My words sting him deeply. I've hurt him, and yet my words seem to have worked. Thank you, Radhika *di*[48]. Now, I understand all those bitter words were just an impetus to make things work out. They were a bitter pill to make our relationship work out.

The doubts all my family members were having were indeed correct. Of course, they have more experience in life than I have. So, they know what's right for me.

Ruhaan confronts his father. Vijay *bhaiya*[4] intervenes and matters get resolved.

The truth is, it was all not that simple for Ruhaan. And what conspired between him and his father, Ruhaan won't tell me. He is just happy. This time, he is not sad after talking to his father.

I pester him to spill the beans, but he won't budge. "Just eat your mangoes, don't count the seeds," he says.

# 27

# Navigating the Waiting Time

**16/07/12**

My patience is being tested. I need to go to the bank, and Ruhaan's parents are demanding a photograph of me. I understand their excitement. The entire family wants to see the girl, the bride-to-be. Ruhaan's mother insists that I must get a latest photo clicked, maybe some shades fairer. Like all Indian mothers, she has dreams of getting the most beautiful bride for his son. But I can't explain this to my family.

I cannot go to the bank or the photo studio right away as I have to visit Radhika *di*'s[48] house to look after her kids. Only then she can go to Ruhaan's house with my family. Ruhaan's parents are demanding a photograph. My family has its expectations, and I am caught in the middle. The situation is complicated.

After completing all the household chores and paying obeisance in the temple, I join my brother on his bike. My brother drops me at his grocery shop, which is in a remote area, promising to return in a few minutes to drop me at *didi's*$_{48}$ house. However, time passes, and there is no sign of him. Frustration sets in as I wait for over an hour. I had planned to go to the bank and get my photograph clicked before going to *didi's*$_{48}$, but I am running out of time. I call him and come to know that he has got stuck in traffic. He suggests I take an auto.

"But where will I find an auto?" I complain.

"You give the phone to Deepak."

Handling the phone to Deepak *Ji*$_{78}$, his employee, I realize my phone has run out of battery. Now Deepak *Ji*$_{78}$, seemingly in his world, leisurely reaches for his phone. Finally, he calls my brother who suggests he help me find an auto. The process is frustratingly slow, testing my patience. Eventually, we find an auto. There is no question of going to the bank or photo studio now. *Bhaiya*$_{4}$ has asked me to reach Sahay's clinic, whence he will take me to *didi's*$_{48}$ house.

Waiting at Sahay's clinic for 45 minutes with a switched-off phone, frustration builds. Eventually, I decide to walk the 15-minute distance to *didi's*$_{48}$ house.

Wait, wait.... it has become my destiny. Wait for everything, first wait for getting your studies completed so that you can get a job, then wait for a good job, then wait for a good match, then leave the job and all your aspirations and dreams, then wait for marriage, wait for everything.

How we humans are victims of our moods. Trifles can aid in ten-folding the frustration when the mood is upset. This week has been a constant struggle, crying and finding faults in my destiny.

Family discussions about the word 'problem' have been ongoing. Sham and I have worked hard to appease both families. My sisters, who were initially in a hurry, are now fretting about the last-minute rush. There is a constant problem with every suggestion. I feel like a burden, unwanted, always waiting. The irony is, while I can wait for my Sham indefinitely, my family can't wait even for a few days. Society's expectations- the same society that never was there during our testing time after my father's death- weigh heavily on my family.

As I reach *didi's*[48] house at 12 pm, my family embarks on a journey to Ruhaan's house, all the ladies draped in *saris*[38] and laden with gold jewellery, despite the scorching heat of July, with sweets and fruits. Tension mounts.

I am on tenterhooks with my heart sinking. 'God, please handle everything, please no fights,' I pray.

Such visions are coming to my mind as if they are all carrying swords in the spirit of a warship. 'What if they fight?' I dread and pray, 'No God, no, don't let this happen,' in the same breath.

Chetan Bhagat is right in asserting in India a marriage is not the marriage of two people, but of two families. And in our case, our families are two different poles.

While my family reacts to everything, Ruhaan's family maintains a reserved demeanour. The real problem is while I am 28, he is just 25; while they can wait and want to wait for 2-3 years, my family can't wait for 2-3 days.

Now look at the irony, while I can wait for my Sham for the whole of my life, my family can't. And that society, in whose name my family wants this marriage to hurry, did it care for my family and me when we were going through the toughest of times after my father's demise?

Not even the so-called dear ones helped, and now this society has become the only concern of my family. I just want to be off my family's shoulders as soon as possible. But in that complete process, I am going to burden Ruhaan's family, forcing myself upon them. *Why don't I suit anywhere?*

"What will people say? It has been so difficult for me to go into society. People ask, don't you want to marry your daughter? Are you going to keep her always? They tell us matches, but we can't answer. What to tell them, that she is having an affair? People wonder, if their girl is good-looking, doing a good job, is coming of age, why aren't they looking for a match? Strange!" My mother has said so many times.

I have been labelled plain and good for nothing since my childhood. And, yet, suddenly I am the most sought-after match. *When and how did it happen?* I wonder! People who injected the inferiority complex in me in a way that I feel instead of blood that complex runs in my veins, are suddenly telling me there is no dearth of matches for me. My mother keeps saying,

"Your two sisters and brother never went like this. Girl, listen. Those who don't listen to their parents always repent afterwards." Though it hurts, she is right. Although I do not get it now, but will understand soon.

*Oh, My God! My brain will burst out. When did not I listen? I have become this today only because I've listened and listened to you utterly. I'd have been a confident person today if I had not listened to you. I'd have been myself, which you never granted me to be. You always used to say, I am not beautiful, it is you who broke my confidence. The fact is, I'm an unwanted child and I'll always remain. The more I try to please you people, the more you get offended,* I want to say, but to whom? Who would understand?

Love, indeed, is blind. Your own family appears enemy to you.

The fact is, all my family members, and I are broken people. We all lost our anchor, the only support. We lost the promise of living a happy, secure life. At least I got to study well. My sisters even didn't get that opportunity. While I feel I am a burden; they want to get rid of me, I understand how my sisters must feel who were married off at very young ages in a hurry. They both were more promising, intelligent, hardworking and outgoing than me. But they never got a chance to build their destiny. None of us got to live the life my father had promised us. My brother, in his teenage years, was burdened with the baggage of caring for two sisters and Mother. He was the only boy to put up with non-medical in our neighbourhood, while all the other boys had dropped out after $11^{th}$. He cracked the entrance, getting admission into prestigious colleges, but despite that, he was not good enough. How could anyone be good enough when life is so unfair to him? So, maybe I am the luckiest one. But right now, I feel miserable, a pang of loss and helplessness tugging at my heart. *Would I have been such a baggage if Papa were alive?* When my sister said that she wouldn't come to my marriage, I started crying and my mother said,

"Why? Do you want to kill us? I am fed up with your crocodile tears. What have we done to you? We care so much. On your wish, we waited for one year. Now what do you want? Do you want to kill us?"

"I am not saying anything," I replied.

"Your sisters never did all this, why……," and mother started screaming in the corner of her *sari*[38], wiping tears and mucus in it.

I didn't reply as I knew whatever I said, they would have something to prove me wrong and blackmail me. They would never give way to me as they are practical people and I am an emotional, sentimental fool, as my sister calls me. I am all heart, Ruhaan says, but still, he loves me.

Why does it happen in India, that if a girl's family has found a match for her, they always remain at the beck and call of the boy's family saying, *'ji ji ji ji'*[73]? Whatever comes out of the mouth of the boy or his family becomes the last word for the girl's parents. But the tables turn if the girl finds a boy for herself. Everything said from the boy's side becomes a topic of discussion in the parliament, and the two families behave like opposition parties. A decision taken by one party is seen with suspicion by the other party. And the boy who otherwise had been the prince at the girl's house, suddenly turns into the worst match for their girl; and the girl, an enchantress who trapped their boy as she couldn't find a match for herself. And the situation becomes funnier if things go as they are going with me. Ironical, but Love is the least considered factor in marriage in our society.

Three and a half years back when I joined IITM College, my family sent my marriage proposal to a boy named Ruhaan working in the same college about which I knew nothing. Look how facts are distorted to find a match. My *jiju*[8] asked an engineer working in some other engineering college to find a match for me and he asked someone else. That 'someone else' who worked in IITM gave the proposal to Ruhaan in this way,

"Ruhaan, do you know Rhythima Ma'am? She is in the Humanities and Applied Sciences Department of our college? Her marriage proposal has come for you. The party is ready to spend five lakh rupees plus a Swift."

So, in the *Baniya*[74] families, a girl's family is not a family, but a party. And the fatter the party, the better the match. Or we can call the girl's family an envelope in Mittal Sir's language.

My family never said a single word about Swift or five lakh rupees. But Prakash Sir made up this story for my sake. I don't know what he was thinking. The boy, on Prakash Sir's suggestion, checked my college profile and when he looked at the date of birth, he said, "No man, she is older than me. Anyway, I'm not planning to marry for the next four years. You know, I'm going to IIT for M. Tech. And after doing M. Tech, I'll do a job. And I'm sure the girl's parents won't wait for four years."

The girl's parents were in no mood to wait even for four months, but God was in full mood.

It has been three and a half years and I am still waiting for him. For the last week, I have been waiting for the day when my destiny has to be decided. There has been complete restlessness since last Monday; I cannot do anything. A rebellion appears to surge through my entire body. My heart refuses to synchronise with the rest of my being. It seems my brain would pop out of my head. I am in no condition to bear any blow by either of the families, not even a single one. Even the clock seems to be at loggerheads with me. It seems it has almost been hours, and it has shifted just one hour. Still, it is 1 in the noon.

'Relax Rhythima, calm down. Whatever will be will be. Moreover, you never asked your mother, *Will I be rich? Will I be pretty?* Good, you didn't ask, otherwise you'd have got a brilliant piece of her mind.'

*God! Am I going nuts? I am talking to myself.*

♥♥♥

**Same day in the evening**

"Congratulations, my wife-to-be."

As the auto jolts, my heart follows suit, almost leaping into my mouth.

"Hey, are you there? I said congratulations."

"W…. what?" I can utter only this.

"What, your family members didn't tell you anything? I hoped they must have told you everything."

"I was at *didi's*[48]; I'm going home now." The noise of the auto hinders clear communication.

"Where are you?" he almost shouts into the phone. His voice, coupled with the auto's clamour, makes my left ear buzz.

"In auto, will be home within half an hour," I reply at my highest pitch.

"You wait; I'll come and drop you," he again shrieks.

"No…. no need. The auto is on its way."

For the first time, I haven't agreed to meet Ruhaan. A peculiar mood has taken hold of me. I should be thrilled. Yet, when he said congratulations, my heart almost sank. Numerous fears surfaced. *So much has already happened; both the families do not match, we two do not match. How will this relationship work out? Is it the right decision? But then to consider any other boy, no I just can't, even the notion scares, so just calm down. Whatever will be will be?* I ponder with the lyrics, *Mera dil bhi kitna paagal hai, ye pyaar to tum se karta hai*[75] playing against the backdrop.

Can the auto*wala*[76] read my face? The song just fits so well!

But some fears refuse to dissipate. Their first condition is I would have to leave my job. I have worked hard my entire life to be independent. Now I am supposed to relinquish that part of myself that I cherish the most. Additionally, there's the matter of cooking; I am not a skilled chef. His father insists on leaving my job and learning household chores, saying to Ruhaan, "Don't let her embarrass us in front of relatives." I will learn everything. After all, what have I done my whole life but please others? *Why are brides chosen on only a few grounds- beauty, complexion, weight and cooking skills? Why is only a fair girl with all the features in perfect proportion considered a suitable match? Why, instead of love, looks become the basis for a match? Why girl's family have to bear everything? Why did you snatch my father from me? Why God, why?* I am at my most vulnerable self right now. So, I afford myself all the negative thinking in the world.

It strikes me as ironic that, after actively contributing to breaking their confidence during their most formative years when they need encouragement, parents blame their children for lacking confidence and zest for life. *How ironic parenting in our country is. I wish I could prepare a course in parenting for Indian parents.* If children receive proper guidance during their formative years, I believe they wouldn't end up as frustrated people pleasers seeking validation from others.

Soon, I will have to relinquish something I love for the sake of love itself- yet another irony. But before bidding farewell to my job, I want to fulfil one last dream of mine that I know I won't be able to pursue again in my life - to make the function of my club, the English Rhetoric Club, a grand success. I have been preparing for it for the past month.

♥♥♥

"The function went exceptionally well. MD Sir called me and my coordinator, and you won't believe what he said. In the five-year history of the college, he has never seen such a function. No teacher has put in as much effort as I did. It was the best function ever. MD Sir, Director Sir, Chairman Sir, all the faculty members–everyone is praising it. I'm so happy," I announce over the phone.

"I always want to see you happy," he replies, revelling in my joy.

"And I'll always be happy with you," I declare, in the highest of spirits.

"Are you sure?"

"Yes! And now, don't start again that your love will diminish over time as you notice my weaknesses," I say, attempting to imitate his tone.

"I know your love will always increase with each passing day, each passing minute," says he, adding, "But won't you miss your job? You have put in so much hard work and earned such a reputation."

"So what? Now I'll work hard to please your parents. I'll earn a reputation there."

"Hmmm."

"Just hmm.... Why don't you say anything when I talk about your family? OK, listen, I am afraid," I grump like a kid.

"Of what?"

"Will your parents like me? I mean, my culinary skills are not that good, and your father wants an expert, doesn't he?"

"Yes, he does. But in the beginning, everyone is a novice, but they learn. You know, my mother didn't even know how to make round *chapatis*[77]. My father used to cut the dough round, rolled by her, with a plate or some lid," he jokes.

"Really?" I am more than surprised.

"Yes."

"Then I am far better. I can make round *chapatis*[77], potato and peas, rice, *pulao*[78], almost all the vegetables," I announce proudly, counting on the fingers of my left hand with the Pinky finger of the right hand. "And guess what? I have learned to make *Suji ka halwa*[79]. You will lick your fingers when you eat *halwa*[79] made by Rhythima. But I am no expert at making any special dishes. Oh God! I still have to memorize the names of *daals*[80]. Don't know what's with these *daals*[80]. Learning everything for me is easy. Don't know why these *daals*[80] make me dizzy?" I sulk again.

"Hey, even I call them yellow *daal*[80], green *daal*[80]. What's the fuss? And don't worry, my mother is an expert; she'll train you."

"How sweet of her. I've even started watching the 'Food Food' Channel. I should leave the job now and be an expert at cooking."

"No, don't leave the job. There's time for marriage, and what will you do after leaving the job? You can't cook all day long, so just keep on doing your job and leave it around marriage."

"How much time is there until marriage?"

"Marriage will take at least six months, but the ring ceremony is decided."

"What?"

"Yes, within a week."

# 28

# Preparing for the Ring Ceremony

The ring ceremony feels more like an exam, evaluating my looks, figure and skills of bending eyes; appearing timid. My soon-to-be- mother-in-law insists on buying the best dress and looking my absolute best. It's a matter of their family reputation, after all.

"Hello, Rhythima," a shrill voice breaks through the phone.

"Um… Namaste m… *Mummy Ji*[81]!"

"Is there anyone around?"

"No…," I respond, climbing the stairs.

"Listen, *beta*[82], tell me if there is any problem. I'm like your mother." The shrill voice makes it challenging to grasp the words falling into my ears.

"Hun."

"Listen, have you started going to the parlour?"

*What?* How do I tell her I have not been to a parlour in my life? I get my eyebrows done from a lady in our village. That's it.

"Listen, you must go to the parlour and take seatings, take a seating daily if required. You know ours is a rrrreputed family, so you must look your bbbbest, you must look ffffair," she says with such an urgency, I get pressurized.

I gulp.

"And buy the bbbbbest dress, the bbbbbest dress, the dress must be eeeeexcellent, you must look eeeexcellent, you must look ssssuperb fair and lovely," she emphasizes, laying stress on the words fair and lovely.

*Don't reputed families have wheat-skinned girls? How would the parlour change my complexion?* I wonder.

"I couldn't tell my mother about this, going to the parlour daily. If I tell her, havoc would happen. What do you say?" I ask Ruhaan.

"Yeah good. She's right, you must take seating," says Ruhaan, somewhat undecided.

There is one week left before my ring ceremony. I am lying in a parlour suggested by a friend. I have been lying down for about two hours with my eyes closed, having no idea what the lady is doing to my face.

The ordeal is over. And when I look in the mirror, I want to shout. I looked much better before. I do not know what she did; I have turned into a blackberry. Yes, I am glowing, but in black. Ruhaan's mother insisted on me looking fair and lovely as it is a question of their reputation.

*Ruhaan, I am sorry, but your family's reputation is at stake now.*

I can't tell anybody at home about the disaster. Thank God, my mother never pays heed to my looks, so she won't know.

I need to buy a dress too, and my mother-in-law is calling incessantly, telling me to look my best and buy the dress from Ambala only.

It's Monday. Mother and I have planned to go to Ambala but, at the eleventh hour, we find out Ambala's market remains closed on Mondays. Radhika *di*$_{48}$ calls me to come and buy the dress from Kurukshetra only. Without telling Mother, I go to her. On the way, I lose my mobile given by Sham to me on my birthday. I am so concerned about my phone that I have forgotten everything about buying my dress.

I try my number from *di's*$_{48}$ phone. The *autowala*$_{76}$ picks up the phone. I had left the phone in auto. The *autowala*$_{76}$ returns it. *Such an honest man. God bless him!* The world has not run out of honest people yet.

Now we enter the garments shop where I buy the very first *lehenga choli*$_{83}$ shown by the shopkeeper, as my sister frets little about clothes. Now she makes me loiter in the entire city with her to find the best *sari*$_{88}$ for herself, which she can't find even after searching the entire market. The idea occurs to her that Ambala is the best place for her to buy a *sari*$_{88}$. After all, she doesn't fret much about clothes.

We reach *di's*$_{48}$ house after buying the *lehenga choli*$_{83}$. My mother-in-law calls her, telling her she wants to come to try some clothes on me. She seems to be a nice lady, always wanting the best for me. I get emotional. But *di*$_{48}$ opens my emotional eyes - the eyes of a sentimental fool.

"You are such a lecher; you are sucking our blood. Why all these dramas? What need to try clothes? I am telling you, only hypocrites do all such dramas, no real people." Radhika *di*$_{48}$ leaves no stone unturned in opening my eyes; the eyes of a sentimental fool. "I'm telling you, if you will do such dramas, I will not attend your marriage." Her BP must have shot up to 140.

"But what have I done?" I cry.

"You always shed crocodile tears. Now why are you crying? Give me my money," she asks for the money she had paid for the *lehenga choli*$_{83}$.

"I'll get it from the ATM and give you."

"Give me my money now," she almost roars.

This is the limit for me, and I leave to get the money from the ATM, covering my face with a *dupatta*$_{60}$, which my *jiju*$_{3}$ despises very much. I cover my face anyway. My mother-in-law is my priority at the moment. On the way, I call Meera *di*$_{48}$, not finding anybody else, and she asks me to come to her place. Going to her means some more scorching heat. But I have no other choice. I had told Ruhaan that I get fair during winters, but keep getting darker as summers approach, especially in July and August. Ruhaan had laughed off the matter, saying, "So, you have colour-changing features." I wish he had taken me seriously and arranged for the ring ceremony in some other month, except July and August. It doesn't seem workable for me to keep his family's reputation during these months. If it were some other months, maybe I could save it.

I decide to go to Chandigarh after paying my sister the money. It takes almost half an hour to reach the ATM. After getting the money, I call Ruhaan on my way back, crying and telling him everything. As I leave *didi's*[48] house with my bag, he meets me after a few steps and takes me to our very own English Department. He tells me his parents are upset, which makes me more upset. I hug him tightly, crying and asking, "What was my fault?" He cannot make out his mother's fault either. Even he suggests that I go to Chandigarh and drop me at the bus stop.

I reach my eldest sister's place burdened by a pressing issue. My complexion! Which has, against my mother-in-law's wishes and in an attempt to fulfil her wishes only, turned magically dark. The darker the complexion, the more Ruhaan's family reputation is at stake. I need to fix this problem. I am trying my best *Saasu Maa*[84] to save your (soon going to be my) family's reputation. You just don't worry, we shall overcome. It feels like the whole nation's feminine gender reputation is on my delicate shoulders. In between all this struggle, I get reminded that the NET Exam date is approaching soon. But I have made a pact with God. I can't pursue my studies and career anymore as it is strongly prohibited for me. Again, it is a matter of Ruhaan's family reputation as girls in the Gupta family have never worked and will never work. So, I have asked God to attribute all the fruit of my hard work- that I've done for UGC NET- and all my prayers to Ruhaan's IES Exam. His happiness is my happiness, after all. Things do not work that way. Soon life is going to teach me. But right now, I am a hopeless romantic. So let me concentrate on this only. *Sacrifice? Oh, I enjoy sacrifice.* We Indian women do, deriving some dark sense of pleasure out of it.

*Didi*[48] takes me to a parlour. The lady promises to solve my problem within two days. Though she has not been able to do much. *Di*[48] calls a *mehndiwala*[85] to apply *henna*[86] on my hands. I am happy, at least not feeling a burden to anybody.

I call the parlour again to confirm the appointment for the day of my ring ceremony.

So tomorrow, I am going to be Ruhaan's fiancé. We, the girl's side, are not supposed to call many of our relatives so I have called none of my friends but one. And that one also cannot come. I miss Naina so much.

We- *didi*[48], *jiju*[3] and their kids reach home in the evening just the day before the ring ceremony. Nobody can sleep - others due to a power cut, me due to excitement and only mother is the one the reason for whose insomnia tonight is me, her daughter.

# 29

# Ruhaan Disposes, Rhythima Proposes

The awaited day has arrived. My brother drops me off at the parlour accompanied by my *lehenga choli*[83] and makeup kit. However, the disapproving glances at my *lehenga choli*[83] from the parlour staff cast a shadow on my excitement. Their knitted eyebrows seem to question, 'What is it?' The sarcasm in their eyes only adds to my melancholy. Alone with my thoughts, I yearn for my two beloved angels, Papa and Naina. My heart aches with longing for them, imagining them watching over me from heaven, Naina all goofy and Papa beaming with love.

'You are not some princess,' I remind myself. 'This is life for you. Remember, you are older and not even beautiful. Just get married and free them.'

Yet, the spirits remain low. To lift my mood, I decide to call Sham. Soon enough, he's by my side.

"Think once more, Rhythima," Ruhaan advises.

"What is there to think?"

"I know how much you love your job and how much hard work you have put in to reach there."

"You know what." I am rising more in love every moment. "I am a warrior, Ruhaan; I am habitual of giving up on my dreams. I had no dreams before you came into my life. But now I have this dream to love and to be loved. I want you, Ruhaan, and a place in the hearts of your family members. If my leaving the job can make them happy, let it be. I love you, Ruhaan. You are my world."

I am head over heels in love. But currently, I fail to realise that sacrificing your dreams for someone else's happiness is not the right way to go. It's not only about quitting the job but so much more. Soon I am going to learn a lot of lessons about life and where I went wrong. Making a person happy is not anyone's responsibility but his/her own. But right now, I am madly in love. Hence, I can't see through all this.

Ruhaan's nose flickers. I know what it means. He is so full of emotions to talk. Right now, all he wants is to cradle me in his arms and shower me with kisses. I tickle his nose, and he falls on his knees. Not to propose, but to dispose.

"Rhyths… I feel… I feel I am not the right person for you. Once you said you don't deserve me, but I know… I… I don't deserve you. I won't be able to provide you with any fancy things… I can't explain it to you… but my family is different. Rhythima. They have called me a loser all my life, you…" he struggles to articulate the words he feels compelled to say, but can't brace himself up. I give him his time. Finally, he blurts out, "You... you marry that doctor."

"Hey, are you on some war with yourself? I mean, why are you so hard on yourself? Any personal rivalry? You are the best thing that has ever happened to me. In Rumi's words, 'I once had a thousand desires, but in my one desire to know you, all else melted away.' And that's true, by the way." I get down on my knees and take his face in my palms, saying, "If not for yourself; do it for my sake; celebrate yourself. Learn to do it, for I am going to do it for the rest of my life. You are my whole cosmos, Sham; my whole damn cosmos, and I mean it when I say it. So, my dear cosmos, learn to love yourself and celebrate yourself. Remember, I won't take a lousy crybaby for my husband. Now get up and cheer up. You are going to get the best girl as your fiancé today. Do you have any idea how lucky you are? I can die for you. And yes, my happiness and dreams are not your responsibility, but mine. I know what I am doing and am happy. So will you now please stop feeling guilty and cheer up?"

"Rhyths, you know what, you are very dominating," he says, feeling lighter now as if a great burden is off his chest.

"I know. Now, will you please leave and let me get ready?"

He rises to his feet, but I remain on my haunches. Then I shift onto one knee and grab his hand. Startled, he turns towards me, and I propose,

"Will you marry me, Mr. Ruhaan Gupta?"

He just nods, tears already pooling in his eyes.

"You need some blusher?" he asks, wiping his tears with the back of his hand.

"What?"

He just covers the distance between us in two long strides, leans down, gives me a peck on the right cheek that makes me blush, and leaves. He does all this in a jiffy. As I turn around to enter the parlour, I find a parlour lady eavesdropping.

"Go on, ask?" I cross my arms over my chest and look her straight in the eye. The girl gets embarrassed.

"I won't take offence; I am ready to satiate any of your curiosities," I probe.

The girl knuckles her fingers. Then she musters up courage and begins, "You know, when you came in to get ready, we made fun of you and your dress."

"I know."

"I am sorry, but I heard everything."

"No problem."

"You… Are you leaving your job for this marriage?" she hesitates while asking.

"Yeah."

"Is it a love marriage?"

"Yeah!"

"But…. I… I mean, the boy doesn't seem mad after you… I mean, he was asking you to marry somebody else. That's strange… does… does he really love you?"

"You won't get his love for me girl... that's deep and pure... so pure where the person doesn't become selfish but is ready to renounce. Like in love, you learn to give and be a better person."

"No pampering and all, ready to die kind of thing... I mean the intensity that *tum sirf meri ho*[87]."

I chortle.

"These are all fancy terms, and for us, love is not a fancy thing, but the most real one that keeps this cosmos going, even amid all chaos. Are you in love?" I wink. She nods. She dials a number on her phone and speaks into it,

"No... no... no, Amit. No, I haven't called for that... no, I am not annoyed. Yes, you don't need to do that. I don't want those crimsons. Yes... no, not even Teddy Bear, and cancel that fancy dinner. It will cost you at least 5000 rupees. *Arre Baba*[88]... no, I am not mad... I love you." The girl gets crimson red.

"Today is my birthday... and I... I," she falters.

"No need to explain. You know there was a time when even I fancied flowers, chocolates, teddies and all. But love taught me there is nothing fancy about it. There is more to love. Flowers wither, chocolates melt, and you will never find the right place for teddies in your home." We both giggle a little. "But you know, love will always find a place; your heart can never fall short of place for it. It blooms with each passing day, with each passing minute. So just keep love intact, nothing else matters. Let love reign and everything else will fall into place."

"Is it that easy?"

"Only we complicate things."

She doesn't seem convinced, but more confident about something. We both enter the parlour.

The lady at the parlour makes me sit with my eyes closed. It has been almost three hours when my phone rings. It is Ruhaan's *mausi*[89] calling.

"*Beta*[82], get ready like a bride, give the phone to your makeup lady."

All are concerned about how I would look, but not me anymore. The makeup lady prepares me like a bride. Meanwhile, both my sisters arrive and my makeup has also been done.

# 30

## It's Time to Pull Your Hair

I am locked in a room at Hotel Saffron. After almost two hours I can see some people, mother and sisters when they come with a cameraman who asks me to make different poses. I am in a fix. *What is going on, and where is Ruhaan?* I have not even talked to him since morning. Nobody seems to approve of my *lehenga choli*[83], makeup, and smile most of all that is too wide for a bride (the special smile Ruhaan has taught me while clicking my photographs). Nothing seems to please them. Or is it I who looks too much for validation? *Shouldn't I be happy rather than bothering about others?* Old habits die hard. It is going to take me years to learn to embrace myself.

I am taken outside. I am instructed to keep my back turned, shielding me from prying eyes until the ceremonies begin. I am asked to go to the stage. As I walk, *bhabhis*[26] and sisters are in shock making strange gestures which I can decode only when I have almost reached the stage. 'Bride running so fast, haw!' the expressions meant.

The cat is out of the bag finally, the bride is visible and most of the guests from Ruhaan's side, who are from IITM, are taken by heels. One of them is Shibhu Sir, a faculty member. Taken aback, he makes a call to his sister, the HOD of the Humanities and Applied Sciences Department, the plot maker for our marriage, the one who assigned the Proctorial Duties in college.

"*Didi*[48], Ruhaan's ring ceremony is going on and you know who the bride is? Rhyyyythima Ma'am."

The already surprised Shibhu Sir is taken aback when the *jaimala*[90] ceremony begins.

"What is this?" he asks my brother-in-law, Aahaan.

"*Jaimala*[90]," Aahaan replies casually.

"But isn't it only a ring ceremony?" asks puzzled Shibhu Sir.

"Yeah, in our families we do *jaimala*[90] in the ring ceremony."

"Strange," he says scratching his scalp adding, "Now, *phere*[24]?"

"Yes, *phere*[24]."

"In…ring ceremony?"

"Yes, we do ring ceremonies like this."

Shibhu Sir almost pulls his hair.

The already fast *Pandit Ji*[91] is bribed to do *phere*[24] faster.

I am Ruhaan's legally wedded wife. It feels like all dreams have come true; Ruhaan is mine means the universe is mine.

So, from now onwards, the Gupta Mansion is my new abode. From a village girl, I have become a city bride; from a Singla, I have become a Gupta- Mrs Rhythima Ruhaan Gupta; the title makes me blush. How a girl becomes a lady, how easily a Singla becomes a Gupta, I used to think. But today I realize it is not that easy. Changing the surname is not an easy job. It means changing your whole being; your whole identity. It means changing yourself upside-down and inside-out. And I am prepared to move heavens to create a place in this home; in Ruhaan's parents' heart. I repeat the two talismans given by Risha in my head. Don't expect them to accept you and don't pretend to be what you are not.

Marriage has happened unplanned, so no rituals are performed, not even those that could be. Ruhaan's father got furious even at the prospect. I feel a little disheartened. I have always loved traditional ways of marriage with all the activities, especially the rituals before and after the marriage. But I revive my spirits, reminding myself that I am not a dotted bride. So, I am ready to put up with everything and be happy. By and by I will make a place for myself here, I kind of decide. Am I not efficient at that?

All the dreams of my hubby have fallen flat on the face, as we cannot share the room. No *puja*[86] has been performed; hence, no meeting.

I am lying in a room, completely new and alien to me with my mother-in-law by my side, wearing a *kurta*[54] of People brand given by my loving mother-in-law as I have entered this home carrying no clothes.

Ruhaan has been taken hold of by some relatives comprising his *bua*[88], *mausi*[89], cousins and their kids downstairs in the hall. He has come to me twice but could not steal a chance to do any mischief.

Finally, he gets a chance. Mother-in-law has gone to take a bath when he comes upstairs to take some plugs. Wasting no time, he comes to me and brushes his lips against mine. A chill goes down my spine, leaving me helpless and wanting more of him. But soon I gather myself as my guard is back.

It was the last visit by him upstairs. I can't sleep the whole night, partly because it is a new place and my mom is not here, and partly because of the chills that are going through my body.

The balloon of excitement about being able to remain with my Ruhaan for the rest of my life gets punctured by the realization that I have to stay in this home for the rest of my life. Tears trickle down as I think of my mother and how lonely she would have been. How lonely she might be; lying alone on her bed. This is the first time she would be so desolate. Only if Papa were there! How selfish I became to be Ruhaan's better half; I didn't think about Mother for once.

Lying there thinking about Mother, all excitement about being Ruhaan's wife gone, suddenly I sit down in bed as I get reminded of Naina's words, the thing you dread the most and desire the most. In all the hullabaloo of marriage, I had completely forgotten about my last meeting with Naina and her last verdict. It seems a sudden realization has dawned upon me. What have I desired all my life? Love and only Love, I know the answer. But do I dread it also? Yes, I do. I do dread losing it or getting it the wrong way.

Now some fears creep in. *Is this love going to last?* I am not lucky about that. And how did Ruhaan persuade his parents? His father especially. He doesn't seem the type who would be threatened, and that is also by Ruhaan. My throat gets dry. I take a peep at Ruhaan's mother. She is fast asleep, like a dead horse. I get out of bed and amble myself over to the kitchen to grab a glass of water. As I am putting the glass in the sink as calmly as I can, a hand comes over my nose and lips, blocking all air. I am about to shriek when I hear a familiar voice,

"Shhhh… it's me."

"Ruhaan?"

"Yes, come with me."

He takes me out of the kitchen; to the balcony and then onto the terrace.

"What are you doing?" I interrogate as soon as we reach the terrace.

"This is not fair," he sulks as he holds my hand.

"What?"

"It is our first night, and I can't even see you."

"Hey relax, don't be a kiddo."

"Yeah, right kiddo, that's why I am dying to feel you." He embraces me.

"Hey Ruhaan, what are you doing? We are in the open."

"But it's dark, relax."

"But what if somebody comes.?"

"No one will come. You don't worry."

Ruhaan takes my face in both his palms. As he tilts my face and comes near, I am about to lose myself. Lost in the moment's magic, I close my eyes when I hear a voice as if someone is clearing his throat. Ruhaan leaves me.

"What's going on here?" a young boy's voice is heard.

"Aahaan, what are you doing here?"

"*Bhaiya*[4], you forgot, you appointed me your guard."

"What kind of guard are you? You are hovering over our heads."

"He is not alone, little mouse," a female voice is heard.

"*Didi*[48]." Ruhaan is in shock on seeing his eldest cousin whom he adores like his own sister.

"Yes me." Ruhaan's cousin comes from behind Aahaan and twitches Ruhaan's ear. "What's going on here? What did *bua*[33] tell you? You can't meet her today."

"Ah…*didi*[48], sorry, I am going." Ruhaan just runs away.

I am standing here, all embarrassed, when *didi*[48] approaches me.

"What are you doing here? You also run," *didi*[48] orders Aahaan and puts her arm around my shoulder, making me sit with her on the folding bed.

"Can't sleep?"

"No!"

"What's disturbing you, child?"

*How does she know? God, you always send someone for me to understand. You are bountiful.*

"Um… How do you know *di*[48]?"

"You know, even mine was a love marriage, so maybe I understand your fears."

"What?"

"Yes… don't be so surprised. Just tell me what's bothering you?"

"U… um… I mean, I don't know what exactly it is?"

*How do I tell her I am tense about how Ruhaan persuaded his father for marriage, and why it was performed unannounced when it was supposed to be only a ring ceremony?*

"You know, Yash *fufa*[93] Ruhaan's father and Maya *bua*[33], Ruhaan's mother, had a love marriage."

"W… what?" It feels like there is no earth beneath my feet.

"B… but he never told me."

"How would he when he didn't know?"

My eyes are like two saucers now.

"I told Ruhaan," *didi*[48] whispers in my ear.

"And?"

"And he used the opportunity, you know, they had to agree. Now don't think too much, just enjoy. OK." She puts a hand on my head.

I come back to the room and lie down on the bed. I am in the same room in the same bed I was a while ago. The only difference is, a great burden is off my chest now. I know my Sham's smile is real, and he is happy. And I am ready for a whole new challenge with a whole fresh energy. If my Ruhaan is happy, I can win this world.

---

The story doesn't end here…

# Epilogue

Rhythima gave up everything, her job, her dreams, and her desires to be Ruhaan's better half. But did it end up with just giving up on her dreams and desires? Was it Rhythima's duty in the first place to make Ruhaan's parents happy? Is it anybody else's duty to make the other person happy? Was Rhythima wrong in deciding to take it upon herself to make Ruhaan's family happy by sacrificing for them? Is there something seriously wrong in the very foundation of our society when it comes to man-woman relationship? Will Rhythima live happily ever after? You might have all these questions popping up in your head. And you will get all your answers in the sequel.

# A Sneak Peek into the Sequel

**2 years later**

"So, how are you feeling today?" The young, dashing psychiatrist in his crisply ironed, blue-striped shirt sits wearing a blank face as he keeps staring at the window on his right side, never turning towards Rhythima.

"Um… OK!" Rhythima gulps. Never does she lift her eyelids as she answers, sitting in the chair across from the psychiatrist who has still not turned to face her.

"So, any better?" The psychiatrist clasps his fingers.

Trying to bat away the image of an octogenarian female doctor that emerges as the psychiatrist clasps his fingers, Rhythima breathes in. "Honestly," she exhales as she answers, "the first four sessions were quite tough. I barely sailed through… them. But I feel better now." Rather than telling, Rhythima seems to be asking, 'Do I feel any better?'

"So, Rhythima." The psychiatrist again clasps his fingers as he turns his chair towards her for the first time, facing her. "Do you have any wish, a strong wish that has always been there?" he asks.

Rhythima's shoulders, which had just relaxed a bit, slump again, her body taut and face contorted. Again, the image of the octogenarian doctor with a silver-pepper head, adjusting her spectacles with her lanky fingers of a hand on which the blue veins are visible, clasping and unclasping them swims in her mind's eye as she looks at the psychiatrist's blank face. *Why does he always wear this blank expression, giving nothing? How does he do it?* Rhythima wonders!

"Look, I know it's hard for you." He rests his clasped hands on the mahogany table in front of him and searches Rhythima's face as he continues, "But you need to tell me everything. So, do you have a wish?"

Rhythima has proved quite stubborn, as she never answers, never ready to open up. The very patient psychiatrist, seeming to lose his cool, especially when Rhythima will not pay him any fees, again turns towards his right side, gazing at the windowsill. Rhythima can sense this. However hard she tries; she always chokes when it comes to speaking emotions. She wants to tell; she does have a wish. That strange wish where she imagines she is engrossed in work when someone, some dear one, comes over and hugs her from behind, surprising her. She wishes there were two open arms only for her in which she can just run and bury her face along with all her worries, all her pain; her loneliness. She longs for a person who doesn't take her breath away, but first makes it go rugged with excitement and happiness and then regular and even.

"Do you remember some particular event, something that keeps coming back to you?" the psychiatrist asks, again trying to be patient, all the while clasping and unclasping his fingers. And Rhythima knows she must answer. She knows the answer.

"Yeah, there is one particular incident." She is fidgeting now, going all nervous and wanting to close again, to go back into her cocoon. The doctor senses it.

"It's OK if the incident disturbs you. Don't mention it, just forget about it."

"No, I… I... I want to share," she replies while breathing, trying to pump in more air inside her lungs.

The doctor sits attentively, his body crisper than his shirt, forearms placed on the mahogany table placed in front of him and spine straight as in a yoga pose. It takes Rhythima some minutes before she begins,

"I was around 6-7. I had gone to Faridabad with my father with some other students of my father's; he was a teacher. He used to take his students to different national-level competitions. He used to take me, too. So, we were in that big stadium roaming around. All the other students were bigger and from sports. Soon, they all began to mount walls and jump outside the stadium. Within minutes, I was the only one left alone there. I was way smaller than them. I was about to cry when I suddenly saw my father coming towards me. And that day…" Rhythima is losing it now. She does not want to speak it, she does not want to admit it, she does not want to accept it. The doctor again turns towards Rhythima and hands her the glass of water that has been sitting all this while on the mahogany table covered with a floral coaster and just sits wearing a blank expression, not giving anything. Rhythima is so intrigued trying to read his expression that her breath becomes regular and she starts talking, "That day when they all gathered at the house crying and wailing, I kept waiting for him. I believed, like that day, he would come opening his arms for me and I'd just run into them. When the whole world would abandon me, he would come for me. He would always be there for me... always. I... I kept waiting and waiting, but he never came." She is shouting now at her loudest; complaining, "He cheated, he cheated. He left me, he left me alone. I had nowhere to go, no one to hold me."

Rhythima is fidgeting, rubbing her face. She is going to break any moment. And this is what scares her, the possibility of losing her calm, of people finding out that her calm exterior is nothing but a facade. On seeing her, who can tell she is so broken?

"And what about your family?"

Rhythima fidgets more, almost on the verge of pulling her hair and running out of this clinic- that seems more like a hotel room with its walls adorned with costly paintings- in the streets screaming, shouting, hollering.

"OK, we won't talk about your family. But didn't you find anyone you could talk to, not even a friend?"

The psychiatrist doesn't expect any answer from her. After all these days, to get that much out of Rhythima is more than he expected.

"There was one," Rhythima speaks as if in a trance. How difficult it is for her to talk about Naina, her Naina in the past tense. She was the one who had taught Rhythima to love herself. She was the one who could read her like the back of her hand. And she was the one who, like her father, had cheated on her, had left her alone in this cruel world. 'I fall upon the thorns of life! I bleed!' she wants to cry but instead tries to put all the emotions that she had felt at the loss of Naina into words.

"I can't… I can't." Her lips tremble, embarrassing her, but she tries, "I can't even bring myself up to form those words. Something about even forming those words in my mouth seems very wrong. I don't want to say those words as if… as if not saying them would change the reality; my only reality; the damn stark reality…" She feels immense anger surging through her as she counts from one to ten. "Reality that can't be changed. Death is the only reality that no indomitable will, no daunting spirit, can change. However hard one may try to run away from it; it will stand there on tip-toes staring you in the eyes; daring you not to accept it. But how dare you? You can't play a stoic when you are at your worst vulnerable self, when your heart is crushed; trodden with a thousand nails; your every belief in God, the supreme shaken to bits."

After a long pause, the doctor says emphatically, "Listen!" Then he thinks. It seems he cannot think of anything. Then again, after a long pause, he asks,

"Do you write?"

"I used to write a blog, but then I stopped when Prabhas…." Rhythima's mind wanders as the image of a sturdy boy with curly hair and a surly smile swims into her mind's eye.

"Resume that." The psychiatrist thinks it better not to dwell on Prabhas, but on her writing.

"What?"

"Resume writing that blog. It will help you."

"Really?"

"Yes!"

"Did you feel happy when you used to write?"

"Yes, ye…, I mean, as long as I got a response from Prabhas and that…" Rhythima trails off.

"Don't look for appreciation. Do it for yourself."

"I feel quite hungry, Rhythima." The psychiatrist clasps his fingers. "You must be hungry, too. Let's take a break." He is up from his chair already. "Meet me here after an hour, OK!" Dr. Patel leaves the room. It takes Rhythima a full ten minutes to calm her nerves down and gather herself up so that she can get up from her chair and grab something to eat. Her stomach churns at the thought of food and she gets reminded she didn't have breakfast. Her last meal was yesterday's dinner of two *chapatis*[77] with four pieces of cauliflower. Not that Rupi is an evil woman who starves her. This is just her way with food and how can Rhythima complain while she doesn't pay any rent?

As Rhythima grabs a doughnut and a cup of coffee, she feels better, in spirits. And within 30 minutes, she is back at her psychiatrist's cubicle. He is already there, in his back-to-business tone. With no formalities, as he has already wasted an entire morning on charity, he starts,

"So, you want to talk about Naina?" As usual, the psychiatrist is facing the window that is to the right side of his cubicle; as usual, clasping and unclasping his fingers.

As usual, Rhythima tries to bat away the image of the octogenarian doctor as she tries to concentrate on the doctor who has not turned to face her yet.

"I have told you about my father and Naina, but I haven't told you about one person." Now the doctor turns towards her, giving Rhythima his full attention. It has become a kind of game for Rhythima, the game of getting the attention of her psychiatrist, the game to get him to turn towards her and look her in the eyes. And to get him to look into her eyes, she must always come up with something; something against her nature; something that is so personal to her that she doesn't feel comfortable sharing it with anyone; something speaking which is threatening to Rhythima. What if it comes true if she says it? But she knows she needs help. Cop uncle says so. He has taken the help of this man with blank expressions.

"So, you were saying you have told me about your father and Naina, but not about one person." The psychiatrist looks Rhythima deep into her eyes, trying to gauge something from in here. And Rhythima enjoys this. She enjoys it when the tables are turned. When it's the doctor, not Rhythima, who is trying to break some code, some silent code. Between Rhythima and the psychiatrist, it goes like this. It's not just the psychiatrist who is trying to break Rhythima's silent codes to help her, Rhythima too is playing that game, although she has not been able to make anything out of the psychiatrist's expressions. But it keeps her involved as long as she stays here in the cubicle.

"Yeah, my husband," Rhythima exhales the air she has been holding all this while as she speaks these words.

"Your husband?" For the first time, Rhythima sees a surprised expression on her doctor's face and she enjoys it. But the psychiatrist doesn't take much time to mask his expression of surprise, as he seems interested.

Again, clasping his hands and turning to the window, he announces, "OK, I am listening."

"I… I have a problem; I can't talk about all… all… this." Rhythima had rehearsed these lines around fifty times beforehand. Still, she stammers as she speaks, "I… I just can't bring myself up to talk about all this."

"OK," the doctor thinks as he speaks, "can you write whatever comes to your mind, whatever you feel, felt at the time you are writing about? You can do this, right?" The psychiatrist again turns towards Rhythima, who has now lost interest in the game.

"Yes!" Rhythima takes a sigh of relief.

“And whatever you feel, write it down.”

“Sometimes I just trail off, not having a cue.”

“OK, we can do one thing. I will ask you questions and you can write their answers like a questionnaire.”

“Um… OK!” Rhythima squares her shoulders.

“But write your answers in detail, with all your emotions and feelings.”

“B… but where should I begin?”

“Um… anywhere, say from the time when things began to, like, um, go downhill in your life… The catastrophe, we… can… say.”

“Should I mail you my answers?”

“Yup, that will be great.”

# Glossary – Exploring the Meanings of Hindi Vernacular Words as Used in the Book's Context.

1. toofani – stormy
2. Chandal Chaukdi – a group of like-minded, fun-loving people
3. Jiju – brother-in-law; sister's husband
4. bhaiya – elder brother
5. Chowk – roundabout
6. panipuris – water balls; a common street food in the Indian subcontinent, it's a deep-fried breaded sphere filled with potato, onion, or chickpea served with water of different flavours like- tamarind, mint, pomegranate, guava, etc.
7. panipuriwala – panipuri seller
8. dabbas – lunch boxes
9. roti – flatbread

10. Jhootha – sipped water
11. chaatwala – Indian street food seller selling lick-tasting delicacies
12. gyaan – knowledge
13. dosa(s) – a type of thin pancake made with ground lentils and rice, originally from Southern India. Dosas are often served with coconut chutney and sambhar
14. idlis – a south Indian cake made from a batter of ground rice and lentils. It is usually served with sambhar
15. samosa (s) – an Indian snack consisting of potatoes, peas and spices wrapped in a triangular pastry case and fried
16. Gulab jamun(s) – a sweet syrupy delicacy eaten in India
17. Mechanchis – a funny term used for Mechanical Engineers to mean they are nothing but mechanics
18. Gopis – female cowherds, lovers of Lord Krishna with whom he dances at the time of autumn moon
19. Kanha – the name of Lord Krishna; an Indian deity
20. mor pankh – peacock feather
21. Dilli abhi duur hai – a Hindi phrase meaning, there is still time

22. chaalu – sly, crafty
23. Arre – oh
24. phere – the ritual of walking of the Hindu bride and bridegroom around a sacred fire
25. O teri ki – oh-my!
26. bhabhi – sister-in-law; brother's wife
27. mama – maternal uncle; mother's brother
28. Aur Sunaiye – Hindi phrase meaning, what's up
29. ullu – nincompoop, idiot
30. Hanuman Ji– a monkey God and a devoted companion of Lord Rama who helped him in his march against Ravana
31. Sai – an honorific title commonly used to address the Indian spiritual master and saint, Sai Baba of Shirdi; a highly revered figure in India
32. Amitabh Bachchan – the most popular star in the history of Indian cinema
33. bua(s) – paternal aunt(s); father's sister(s)
34. dadi – grandmother
35. chacha Ji – paternal uncle; father's younger brother
36. yaar – a friend; a term often used between males in direct address

37. salwar kameez – a type of suit, worn especially by Asian women, with loose trousers and a long shirt

38. sari(s) – a long piece of cloth that is wrapped around the body to make a long dress, worn by women in South Asia; traditional dress of women of India

39. Accha – okay

40. Diwali - a Hindu festival held in honour of Goddess Lakshmi, the goddess of wealth. It is celebrated in October or November with the lighting of lamps in homes and temples, and with prayers to Lakshmi Ji.

41. Haldiram - an Indian multinational sweets, snacks and restaurant company

42. namkeen – a salty snack or savoury

43. rasgulla(s) – popular Indian sweet made from ball-shaped dumplings of curdled milk

44. rice and curry – a staple Indian dish made of rice served with curry, a sauce or gravy flavoured with a complex combination of spices and herbs

45. Maa – mother

46. Na Baba Na – emphatic way of saying 'no' in response to a question or statement

47. jhingalala hur – when a person is in a jolly mood this word explains his/her happy gesture and tells that all is good. This word is mostly used by the tribal community when they find their prey

48. didi/di – elder sister(s)

49. Bhondu Ram – artless person, naïve

50. main kaa karu Raam mujhe Bhondu mil gaya – what should I do God, I've found a simple, naïve person who is utterly artless

51. jaan - beloved

52. dadaji – grandfather

53. Aashiq Sahib – lover boy

54. kurta – a long loose garment like a shirt worn in India

55. Ranjha Ranjha kardi ve main aape Ranjha hoi… mainu Heer naa aakho koi - famous Bollywood song meaning, calling out for Ranjha (beloved) for so long, I've myself become Ranjha. Call me Ranjha now, don't call me Heer anymore

56. Jaise filmon mein hota hai, exactly waisa hi is happening to me, zubi doobi zoobi doobi – It's happening like it happens in the movies (famous Bollywood song from the movie Three Idiots)

57. Om Namah Shivay – a devotional chant that translates to 'I bow to Shiva.' Lord Shiva is a principal Hindu deity

58. karma – (in Hinduism and Buddhism) the sum of a person's good and bad actions in this and previous states of existence, viewed as affecting their future

59. pink dupatte me kya haseen lag rahi ho – you are looking ravishing in a pink dupatta

60. dupatta – a length of material worn arranged over the chest and thrown back around the shoulders, typically with a salwar kameez by women of India

61. Kithe challe sonyo gobi daa phool banke – where are you going looking so beautiful

62. Teri Meri Kahani – A Bollywood movie title meaning, your and my story

63. kahani – story

64. Brahmastra – ultimate weapon

65. Rimjhim rimjhim, runjhun, runjhun, bhigi bhigi rut mein tum hum hum tum, chalte hain – romantic Hindi song on rain meaning, pitter-patter, pitter-patter/ in the season of rains/ you and I, I and you/ we'll walk together

66. Jahaan – universe

67. bahu – dauther-in-law

68. sarvgun samppan – bestowed with all the great qualities

69. Sati Savitri – chaste, virtuous, pious lady dedicated to her husband

70. ghazal – the most popular genre of Urdu poetry sung with music and rhythm

71. mandap – pavilion temporarily erected for the purpose of a Hindu or Jain marriage

72. dabbu – submissive, timid, tame, pretty meek fellow

73. Ji – used to denote respectful attention; a suffix placed after a person's name or title as a mark of respect

74. Baniya – an Indian cast consisting generally of moneylenders or merchants, found chiefly in northern and western India

75. Mera dil bhi kitna paagal hai, ye pyaar to tum se karta hai – Bollywood song meaning, how mad my heart is that it loves you

76. autowala – autorickshaw driver

77. chapatis – a type of flat round Indian bread

78. pulao – a rice dish cooked with vegetables and hot spices

79. Suji ka halwa – it's a sweet dessert made from semolina, sugar, ghee (clarified butter), and often flavoured with cardamom and garnished with nuts

80. daal(s) – pulse(s)

81. Mummy ji – mother-in-law

82. beta – an endearing term used by elders for the younger ones; also, son

83. lehenga choli – a type of ethnic clothing worn by Indian women usually on ceremonial occasions

84. Sasau Maa – mother-in-law

85. mehndiwala – the person who makes designs with henna

86. henna - a reddish-brown dye that is made from the leaves of a shrub. It is used especially for colouring hair or skin

87. tum sirf meri ho – you are only mine

88. Arre Baba – oh, man!

89. mausi – maternal aunt; mother's sister

90. jaimala - a well-known ritual during a Hindu wedding, where a bride and a groom exchange garlands, as an indication of acceptance of each other as their spouse, and a pledge to respect them throughout the rest of their lives

91. Pandit Ji – priest

92. puja - a ritual in honour of the Gods, performed either at home or in the mandir (temple)

93. fufa – paternal uncle; husband of father's sister

www.ingramcontent.com/pod-product-compliance
Lightning Source LLC
LaVergne TN
LVHW041159150826
845673LV00001B/222

*9798892778282*